D0288316

A King Production presents…

Young Diamond Books
PRESENTS
A young adult urban tale

Ride Wit' Me

A Novel

DEJA KING

This novel is a work of fiction. Any references to real people, events, establishments, or locales are intended only to give the fiction a sense of reality and authenticity. Other names, characters, and incidents occurring in the work are either the product of the author's imagination or are used fictitiously, as those fictionalized events and incidents that involve real persons. Any character that happens to share the name of a person who is an acquaintance of the author, past or present, is purely coincidental and is in no way intended to be an actual account involving that person.

ISBN 10: 0975581198
ISBN 13: 978-0975581193
Cover concept by Deja King & www.MarionDesigns.com
Cover layout and graphic design by: www.MarionDesigns.com
Typesetting: MarionDesigns
Edit: Linda Williams, Dolly Lopez and Suzy McGlown
Library of Congress Cataloging-in-Publication Data;
King, Deja
Ride Wit' Me: a novel/by Deja King
For complete Library of Congress Copyright info visit;
www.joykingonline.com

A KING PRODUCTION

P.O. Box 912, Collierville, TN 38027

A King Production and the above portrayal log are trademarks of A King Production LLC

Copyright © 2009 by Deja King. All rights reserved. No part of this book may be reproduced in any form without the permission from the publisher, except by reviewer who may quote brief passage to be printed in a newspaper or magazine.

This Book is Dedicated To My:

Family, Readers and Supporters. I LOVE you guys so much.
Please believe that!!

Acknowledgments

As always I want start off by thanking ALL of my readers and supporters. I truly feel blessed to have readers that show me so much love. I will forever be humble and grateful. I love you all so much...please believe that. Hugs and Kisses!!

Your Literary Sweetheart,

Deja "Joy" King

Special Thanks To...

Linda Williams, Tracy Taylor, Tazzy, Keith Saunders, Ann Hopson, Rahman Muhammad of The Book Bullies and my girl Jonesy!!

Tureko "Virgo" Straughter, Renee Tolson, Jeanni Dixon, Ms KiKi, Andrea Denise, Sunshine716, Ms. (Nichelle) Mona Lisa, Lady Scorpio, Travis Williams, Brittney, Donell Adams, Myra Green, Leona Romich, Sexy Xanyell. To vendors and distributors like African World Books, Teddy Okafor, Black & Nobel, DaBook Joint, The Cartel, DCBookman, Tiah, Vanessa and Glenn Ledbetter, Junior Job, Anjekee Books, Urban Xclusive DVD & Bookstore, Future Endeavors. Also, to Yvette George,

Velva White, Thaddeus Matthews, Sherita Nunn, Troy Monaco, James Davis, Marcus & Wayne Moody, Ann Hopson, Trista Russell, Risque Café, Don Diva, Dolly Lopez and Jonesy... thank you all for your support!!

Special, special thanks to Cover 2 Cover Book Club; Christian Davis, Angela Slater, Pamela Rice, Ahmita Blanks, Melony Blanks, Marcia Harvey, Melinda Woodson, Tonnetta Smith, Tiffany Neal, Miisha Fleming, Tamika Rice and Bar. I so enjoyed our book chats for "Hooker to Housewife" and "Superstar". All of you ladies are wonderful!!

Ride Wit' Me

Chapter 1

Daddy's Little Girl

The first lesson I remember my daddy teaching me was, "Mo' money, mo' problems." It seemed everyday he would walk around the house screaming those exact words.

One day when I was six years old, I was sitting in the kitchen finishing up my Captain Crunch cereal, and my dad came in yelling at someone on his cell phone. When he finished the call, he slammed his phone on the counter and growled, "Mo' money, mo' problems."

I gulped the last bit of my milk and said, "Daddy, you're always saying, 'Mo' money, mo' problems'. What does that mean?"

He sat down next to me and twirled one of the Shirley Temple curls in my hair like he always did when he spoke to me up close and personal. "Mercedes, look around you," he said, as his long muscular arm reached out as if presenting a gift. I glanced around, following Daddy's arm. Then I turned back to him with big inquisitive eyes. "Baby girl, everybody don't live like this. All this marble, high ceilings and 24k gold encrusted fixtures, spell nothin' but mo problems."

"If it causes you so many problems, then why do we have it?"

"Because this is the only life I know, and the only life I want you and your mother to have. But, the mo' money you make, the mo' problems you gonna have. All this comes with a high price," he said as he held my chin up and looked me directly in the face. "But, baby girl, you're worth it."

For the next ten years, I lived what most would consider the ideal life. I was chauffeured around in the most expensive cars. I had a closet full of designer clothes, my very own platinum credit card, and went on vacations to exotic islands that you only heard about on travel networks. I attended exclusive private schools, and by all accounts, my life was perfect. My parents adored me, especially my daddy. I was his little girl. Although I no longer looked liked a little girl, in his eyes, I would always be.

It wasn't until the summer of 2006, when I turned sixteen, that my world turned upside down and it became clear to me what my dad meant by "Mo' money, mo' problems."

As I did every year, I left my uppity boarding school in Wallingford, Connecticut, and came home to Illinois. I always looked forward to getting away from the rich and privileged white kids and coming home to kick it with my cousin, Keisha. She was my first cousin from my mother's side of the family. With her, I could keep it real. There was no being uptight and perfect. Although I detested being around the rich and privileged, I was one of them too. The only difference was that I didn't take it so seriously. Yeah, I knew my family had paper, and when it came to material items, I never heard the word "no". But beyond that, by no means did I walk around like my "ish" didn't stink, because at the end of the day, it did, just like everybody else's. My toilets just happened to be made of gold, that's all.

When the limo pulled up to the winding driveway leading to my family's estate, encompassing well over 20,000 square feet, I was more excited than usual about being home. My sixteenth birthday was a couple weeks ago, and I always had a birthday party the upcoming weekend I returned home.

The kids on MTV's "Sweet Sixteen" had nothing on me. My parents would go all out— more likely, my dad. When I was a little girl, he would turn our backyard into an amusement park. As I got older, he would come up with more sophisticated surprises. Last year, he had Chris Brown perform, and actually had the stage looking as if he was dancing on top of a pool of water. And the year before that, he had Omarion. When it came to me, there was nothing my dad wouldn't do. Now that I was sixteen, there was no doubt he would be blessing me with an official ride. I just hoped he would get the car of my dreams, and not his.

I sat in the limo for a moment, staring at our mansion that sat on five acres in Northfield, on a private cul-de-sac surrounded by iron gates and a state-of-the-art security system. The exquisite architectural masterpiece was comprised entirely of stone and brick with intricate detail work.

The driver opened the limo door. I walked towards the solid mahogany doors and stepped in the circular foyer with cherry trim, limestone flooring, and a soaring mahogany ceiling, which always made a dramatic first impression. It was very quiet, and the bodyguards weren't standing at their usual post.

Right when I was about to call out to my moms, everyone ran into the foyer and screamed, "Surprise!"

I was totally stunned to see all my friends and family members appear like magic. Well actually, my friends were my blood family and the people who worked for my dad. No one outside of that circle was allowed into our home. My dad was a strong believer in that. He had a whole army working for him, and I never quite understood what their job positions entailed or exactly what my dad did for a living. When I would inquire, my parents would only say that he was a successful entrepreneur. In school I learned what an entrepreneur was, but none of them seemed to live the lifestyle that I was accustomed to, so instead of letting my curiosity grow, I just accepted that my family was different.

"I can't believe y'all threw me a surprise birthday party! I wasn't expecting this!" I squealed, truly in shock.

"That's why it's called a surprise, baby girl." Daddy was the first to walk over to me, and he planted a kiss on my forehead. "I'm so proud of you. My little girl is growing up."

When I looked up at him, I actually saw a slight trace of tears in his eyes. No one else would've noticed, but I did.

"Girl, you're sixteen, and we gon' have the summer of a lifetime," my cousin, Keisha hummed while snapping her fingers and grinding her hips.

I noticed my dad giving Keisha the disapproving eye. He always claimed that she was entirely too grown. I was just as grown, but I knew to do all that booty shaking behind closed doors. That was the difference between my cousin and me. She simply had no shame in her game.

"Mercedes, you look absolutely beautiful. Just look at my baby." My mother turned me around, observing my five foot seven, hundred and twenty-five pound curvaceous figure. I had to admit that I was indeed a beauty. But how couldn't I be with parents like mine? If my mother hadn't met my dad when she was fifteen and settled down with him, she could've easily been a fashion model. She had the delicate bone structure and flawless caramel skin that any super model would envy. And my dad was a few inches taller and a younger, more handsome version of Denzel Washington. I know that might sound impossible, but if you saw him, you'd be a believer.

"Moms, would you stop! You're embarrassing me!"

My mother was making me blush, because by this time, my whole family was surrounding me. I was my parents' only child, and the majority of my family consisted of boys, so I constantly felt as if everyone put me on an uncomfortable pedestal. By no means was I shy, but an overwhelming amount of attention could quickly become irritating to me.

For the next few hours, we all ate and partied as if we were having a New Year's celebration. Then my dad had the DJ put on Luther Vandross' Dance with My Father. All the partygoers cleared the dance floor as my dad grabbed my hand and led me to the center of the room. He held me close and whispered in my ear as we slow danced to the music, "A father couldn't have asked for a more perfect daughter than you. You will always be Daddy's little girl."

Chapter 2

Love At First Sight

When I woke up the next morning, I was still smiling from the fabulous party my dad had given me. Even though there weren't any celebrity performances or rollercoaster rides, it was still the best birthday party of my life. I finally felt as if I was becoming my own person, with an identity outside of being Ronald Clinton's daughter.

When I looked over beside me, I noticed that Keisha was still knocked out. Although we had more than enough guest bedrooms, Keisha and I always slept in the same bed when she came to visit for the summer. Most of the time we would stay up until the middle of the night, laughing and gossiping about what took place the previous school year. Keisha's stories were always more interesting than mine. She lived in New York, and the drama that took place there was definitely over the top. I often wished that I went to a public school and was able to kick it with just regular kids who weren't so pretentious.

I was starving, so I let my cousin sleep and went downstairs for breakfast. I could smell French toast and home fries in the air. My stomach began growling at the thought of tasting butter and syrup over my French toast. We had an in-house cook, but nobody could fix my favorite breakfast like my mother. It was a ritual for her to make my favorite meals whenever I came home.

"Good morning, birthday girl!" my mother smiled, and sipped her mimosa.

"It's not my birthday anymore."

"Says who?"

"The calendar."

"Oh, please! You know your father ain't done with you."

"What you mean, Ma?"

"I ain't saying nothin' else. Your father will be down here any minute. He'll tell you. You know how things have to be in a certain order with him."

That was a nice way of my mother saying that my dad was a complete control freak, which he was. His hands had to touch everything, from the most minor things to the biggest.

"Well, while we're waiting for the 'King's' arrival, I'm 'bout to demolish this food."

By the time I was on my second serving, my dad graced us with his presence. As always, he was immaculately dressed, as if on his way to a business meeting. He walked over and kissed my mother on the lips and playfully patted her behind.

My parents had been together for over sixteen years, but they still acted like two teenagers in love. I prayed that one day I would find love like that. The only thing that annoyed me about their relationship was that my mother always seemed to bow down to my dad. Whatever he says, goes. She wouldn't dare question his decisions or give her opinion, even when it was written all over her face that she disagreed. I guess because he swooped her up when she was so young, her mind was pretty much programmed to obey his every word.

"How did my baby girl enjoy her birthday party?"

"It was incredible, Daddy! I had the best time. Thank you so much!"

"We'renotfinishedyet. Unfortunately,itwasn't ready yesterday, but it arrived early this morning."

"What arrived?"

"Go out front and take a look."

When I walked outside and saw the custom-made white-on-white drop top CLK 500, I started screaming as I jumped up and down. My dad did me proud and got me the car I wanted. See, I just knew he was going to cop me some kind of truck. He was always stressing that I didn't need a sports car or a convertible.

I guess my loud mouth woke Keisha up, because the next thing I heard was her screaming, and when I turned around to see where the raucous was coming from, she too was jumping up and down.

"Yo, I can't believe Uncle Ronny got you this fly whip! You betta work it! Every dude in Chi-town is gon' be sweatin' us. On the real, let's shower, get dressed and be out."

"You ain't said nothin' but a thing. Let's do it, 'Thelma'!" Those were our nicknames. Keisha was Thelma, and I was Louise.

Before heading upstairs, I ran to my dad and gave him the biggest hug. "Daddy, I love you so much! This really is the best birthday ever!"

"I love you too. Now you and Keisha better not get in any trouble out there. I don't need to warn you that just as fast as I gave you that car, I can take it away."

"I know, Daddy. But do you really have to threaten me? I mean, darn, I haven't even driven the car yet!"

"Sorry, baby girl. I just worry about you. Enjoy yourself." He gave me a kiss, and I sprinted upstairs.

By the time I reached my bedroom, Keisha already had her outfit laid out on the bed and was in the shower. She planned on rocking her extra short-shorts. I pulled out my cream Juicy Couture embroidered off the shoulder top and matching shorts from their new haute couture collection. The outfit was like that, and would shine perfectly with my new drop top.

"Girl, that's what you wearing today?" Keisha asked, smacking her lips while eyeing my outfit.

"You know it! Don't hate 'cause my outfit is pure fi-ya!"

"Miss Thing, you already know I'm 'bout to hate. We've been goin' through this every summer since we were eight years old. You always had the best dolls, the newest games, and the flyest clothes. Ain't nothin' changed."

It was no secret that Keisha was envious of the life I lived, and I appreciated that she never fronted about it. And every summer when she would leave, I would end up shipping her a ton of stuff that she begged me for, since there weren't enough days in the year for me to wear half of them.

"Well, I can't let you rock this joint here. When we go to the mall today, I got you for a couple of outfits." I winked my eye at Keisha as I reached in my purse and pulled out my credit card.

"Ah, show me what's really good! That's right, cuz!" Keisha gave me a pound as I walked towards my bathroom to take a shower.

Forty-five minutes later, we were headed downstairs to begin our summer, cruising around in my new ride.

"Where are you going in that outfit?" I heard my dad bark.

I thought he had already left the house to start his day, and I wasn't in the mood for a lecture. I put on my sweetest voice so I could hurry the conversation along. "Daddy, what's wrong with my outfit? Mommy is the one who got it for me."

My dad turned and ogled my mother, who was sitting down skimming through her Essence magazine. She didn't look up to acknowledge my dad's glare in an attempt to pretend she didn't hear him.

"Latoya, I know you didn't buy Mercedes that outfit," he finally said, after growing tired of the silence. Normally my dad called my mother "Toy" for short, so when he called out her full name, we all knew he was serious.

"When I was at Neiman's, I thought the outfit was beautiful and would look very cute on Mercedes. I'm sure she wouldn't mind taking it off if you don't approve."

"Yes, I would!" I belted. I wasn't surprised my moms took the sucker way out. She never wanted any beef with my dad. "Daddy, I love this outfit, and there's nothin' wrong with it. Look at Keisha. Her shorts are way shorter than mine. Please don't ruin my birthday weekend, Daddy."

My dad stared me up and down, and then glanced over at Keisha. Luckily, her shorts were on the hoochie side. In comparison, it made my shorts look as non-sexy as your grandmamma wearing a pair of bloomers.

"Alright, I guess they ain't that bad. You girls be careful, and I don't want any boys in your car. You hear me?"

"Of course, Daddy. You don't have to worry. No boys, I promise." I gave him a kiss and walked off with Keisha.

"Bye, Mercedes!" I heard my mother yell out as I reached the door. I gave her a shady bye back.

"My moms kills me. She gets on my nerves, always keeping her mouth shut when it comes to my dad. She never defends me."

"Yeah, but she's so in love with Uncle Ronny, she turns into mush when it comes to him."

Choosing to put my moms out my head, we hopped in my Benz, put the top down, and I pulled out my Alicia Keys CD. Right before I drove off, I placed my clear Christian Dior rhinestone shades on my face for the finishing touch.

We headed to Northbrook Court to do some shopping, and I felt like an R&B diva as the wind blew through my hair. The summer breeze made me want to head towards the beach and lay out in a two-piece bikini. "Before the summer's out, we need to go to Miami or somethin' and lounge on the beach," I said.

"Yeah, girl, and maybe meet a rapper or somethin'. When I be listening to the Morning Show on Hot 97, they always talkin' about how all the celebrities be chillin' over there," Keisha said.

"For real?"

"Umm-hmm. I wouldn't mind hookin' up with Souljah Boy. He's such a cutie."

"He's cute, but I think that dude, Dwayne Wade is sexy," I said.

"Who in the world is Dwayne Wade?" Keisha asked.

"A basketball player. He plays for the Miami Heat."

"Oh. Besides Allen Iverson, basketball players don't be thugged out enough for me. I like me a roughneck."

"Some things never change, and you one of them."

When we finally arrived at the mall, it was jammed packed, which was to be expected for a Saturday afternoon.

"Why don't you do valet parking?"

"Because I don't feel like paying no valet money. Plus, there's a parking spot right there." I pointed over to a prime parking space that I noticed someone about to pull out of.

"Hurry up and get that, 'cause that's right by the entrance and I don't feel like walking."

"You so lazy. But I got this." I headed over to the spot, and out of nowhere, this Range Rover pulled up and stole my spot. "That's really 'hood. Where did that car come from?"

"I don't know, but check out the rims on that ride. Those look like 24's."

"I don't care about all that, I want my parking space. I need to get the driver's attention, but the tint on the windows is too dark."

I started blowing my horn, and a guy on the passenger side stuck his head out of the window. "What's the problem?" he asked.

"The problem is that you're in my parking space."

"Oh, my fault, shorty. You can have the spot."

Keisha and I both looked at each other, thinking that this was easier to handle than we thought.

"Thanks, I appreciate that."

"All you gotta do is show me where your name is written that this spot is reserved for you."

My blood started to boil. This baby faced looking

boy wanted to get slick with the tongue. I knew it all seemed to be going too smoothly. "Listen, my name isn't written anywhere."

"Oh, so technically this isn't your parking space. Then we gon' stay right here."

"I was here first, and y'all just rolled up and took this spot. That's foul."

Right when I was about to start spewing off some four-letter words, the finest boy I had ever seen in my life came walking around from the driver's side. At that moment, the parking space or the smart talking boy was irrelevant. I fell into a trance. It was love at first sight. It wasn't until Keisha started nudging my arm that I began to snap out of it.

"Girl, I can imagine how you feelin' right now, but honey, don't let him know it," she warned.

She was right. I wanted to scream, "Screw the parking space, if you would please just give me your digits!" but I had to keep my self-control.

"What seems to be the problem?" my dream guy asked with the calmness of the most peaceful waters.

"Me and my cousin just wanted to have a nice day at the mall celebrating my birthday, and now it's been ruined because y'all basically stole my spot. And your slick at the mouth friend here just tryna make it worse."

I peeped his friend's mouth open as if he was about to go at me for round two, but my dream guy put his hand up, letting him know to chill. He looked no more than eighteen, but his whole aura was that of a grown man. He possessed a type of confidence and gave off the energy of being "The Man".

"I apologize for disrupting your day. I'll have my man move the car and you can have the parking space."

His friend was shaking his head, furious that he made me the offer, but held his tongue as if he knew better to speak on it.

"You would do that for me?" I asked, sounding surprised.

"Without a doubt. But in exchange, can you do somethin' for me?"

"Whatever you want." When the words left my mouth, I hoped they didn't sound as desperate as I felt.

"Let me take you out for your birthday."

The invitation leaving his delicious lips was music to my ears. I knew I should've played high post and not so easy to get, but it was like I couldn't help myself. "Just let me know when."

He gave me a perfect smile that should've been on one of those, Got Milk commercials. "Demetrius, take the car to the valet so this young lady can have her parking spot."

His friend did as he was told, and I pulled into the space.

Girl, that cat is so fine, and he's feelin' you. Do you think that's his ride?" Keisha asked.

"I don't know, and I don't care. He's so cute, he could be walkin' and I'd still give him the digits."

"Okaaaay!"

Right when I was about to step out of the car, my dream guy opened the door for me. "You didn't have to do that."

"I know. I wanted to."

"Thank you." I could tell I was blushing and I put my head down, feeling silly for being dumbstruck over a dude I didn't even know.

"So, you a daddy's little girl?"

"Excuse me? Where did that come from?" I asked, obviously taken aback by his comment. I knew I had never laid eyes on him before, so how would he even know or think something like that?

"Your vanity plates."

I stood there for a moment, still confused.

"On your car. That's what the tags say. This is your car, right?"

"Yeah, I actually just got it today as a birthday present. I haven't even checked out the plates." This guy must think I'm a complete moron, I thought to myself.

"It's nice. You really must be a daddy's little girl."

"No, I'm not!" I snapped. For some reason, his comment was making me feel so childish, and I wanted to feel like a young woman.

"There's nothing wrong with being a daddy's girl. I think it's cute."

And just like that, all my insecurities went out the window. He made me feel like I was special.

"So, can I hang with you at the mall, or will I be cramping you and your cousin's style?"

"Of course you can hang with us!" I responded quickly.

"Cool."

"Just to let you know though, we're shopping, so don't be tryna rush us out the stores," Keisha added, not wanting my new crush to interfere with the new outfits I promised her.

"I don't have a problem with that. I just want to spend some time with your girl. My fault. I don't even know your name."

"Mercedes."

"I guess your pops already knew what type of whip

he planned to cop you since the day you were born."

"Funny! What's your name?"

"Dalvin, but my friends call me D."

"Then I'll call you Dalvin."

"Only my mother calls me Dalvin, but I'll make an exception for you."

This dude had me straight tripping. I didn't know if it was his mesmerizing eyes that put Terrence Howard's to shame, or his low cut loose curls that I was dying to run my fingers through. Or maybe it was his lean muscular body that was highlighted by his reddish brown complexion. Whatever it was that sunny afternoon in front of Northbrook Court, I fell in love for the first time in my life.

Chapter 3

Kisses Don't Lie

That afternoon at the mall, Dalvin, and surprisingly his friend, were perfect gentlemen. They escorted us around the stores and held our bags as I blew up my credit card.

Keisha picked out a few fierce outfits, and Dalvin even bought me a dress as a birthday present, even though I begged him not to. He insisted on getting it for me, claiming that he thought the dress was banging and wanted me to wear it on our first date. But then to take it a step further, while I was window shopping at the Louis Vuitton store, he purchased a purse to go with the dress he bought.

Keisha and I kept looking at one another in amazement. For one, I didn't understand how he could afford such pricey items at his age. When I asked him, he said, "Just like you're daddy's little girl, I'm my father's only son. As far as he's concerned, the world is mine."

That bugged me out. Going to my prep school, I saw a ton of rich white boys whose fathers' treated them that way, but I never heard a black guy say something like that. I guess if my dad had a son, he would be the same way, but he didn't. He only had me.

After four hours of strolling around the mall and getting something to eat, Keisha realized that not only was Demetrius cute, but also rather sweet, so they started kicking it.

"So, where are you telling your parents we're goin' tonight again?" Keisha asked as we got dressed for our dates with Dalvin and Demetrius.

"I'm going to tell them the truth that we're goin' to the movies and out to eat. I'm just gonna leave out the part that we won't be solo, but accompanied by two guys."

"That works for me. But if you and D start really feelin' each other, then will you tell your parents that you found a boyfriend? I mean, my goodness, you are sixteen. My moms started lettin' me date when I was fourteen."

"I don't think my mother would have a problem with it, and neither should my dad. I mean my mother was pregnant with me at my age. But you know how my dad is. He's gonna want to take fingerprints, urine samples, the whole nine if he even thinks a guy is breathing in my space. So I'll have to space this one out."

"I feel you, but I got a feelin' very soon you and D will be a couple. Homeboy seems like he's really feelin' you. Y'all was holding hands and walking through the mall like you'd been together for years."

"I know, right? That's how he makes me feel, like I've known him forever. Don't laugh. I already think I'm sprung."

"Nah, it's more than you think. You definitely are. But who could blame you? He's crazy cute, and he seems like he's livin' betta than Bow-Wow, without dropping an album or being in videos. I can't help but wonder who his daddy is."

"I was thinking the same thing. His family lives in Chicago, and I wonder if his father knows my dad. Or better yet, if they do business together. If they do, that would be even better. My dad always says that most of his business associates are like family to him. So dating Dalvin would be all good."

"That would be sweet if it worked out like that. I mean, your family got long paper, and it seems like D's family does too. So, if y'all merge the families, y'all be runnin' Illinois."

"Keisha, you so dramatic. This ain't no mob movie."

"I know, but it sounds good though."

When Keisha and I left to go out, luckily my dad was gone and my mother was the only one home. She loved for me to dress up and go out. She always wanted me to have a good time, but would chicken out in front of my dad and never express that.

When we got to the movie theater, the guys had already got our tickets to the movie.

"Mercedes, you look gorgeous. I knew you would look perfect in that dress," Dalvin said, running his fingers through my shoulder-length jet-black curls. I used the opportunity to do the same to his hair, since I had been dying to do so. His hair was just as soft as mine.

"Y'all look like brother and sister standing over there," Keisha remarked with a chuckle. She was right though. We could've easily passed for siblings, but thank goodness we weren't.

After the movie, we went to P.F. Chang's for dinner, and all of us just cracked jokes and bugged out. I was having so much fun and couldn't believe how fantastic my summer was starting off.

After dinner, we followed behind Dalvin and Demetrius as they drove to this roller skating rink that a lot of teenagers hung out at. The parking lot was packed, and it seemed more people were hanging outside than inside. I parked my car next to Dalvin's and leaned against the Range with him as he pumped Jay-Z's CD. Mad heads were coming up showing him love.

"You know everybody," I commented.

"No, I don't know everybody, but everybody knows me," he laughed. I gave him a playful smack over his head.

"You never told me how old you are," I inquired.

"Just a year older than you."

"Wow, you already gettin' so much respect, and you're so young!"

"Young is as young do. So, I ain't been young in a minute, because I do very grown things."

"Like what?"

"I do a lot of work for my father. You can say he's grooming me to one day run the family business."

"What type of business does he run?"

"A combination of things. You can just call him a very successful entrepreneur."

In that instant, a light flashed in my head, that was the same way my parents described what my father did for a living. Maybe Dalvin's dad and my dad did work together. Right when I was about to ask him his father's name, I noticed a small crew of girls walking towards Dalvin and I. Keisha peeped them and immediately headed over in my direction.

"What's up, D? Why haven't you returned my phone calls?"

"I've been busy. And as a matter of fact, I'm busy

right now."

"Busy doing what? It's summer time. You can't get no extra credit for tutoring little girls," she said sarcastically. She and her friends all broke out laughing at my expense.

"I ain't no little girl!" I cracked, ready to punch the Megan Goode knockoff.

She began mocking me as her friends egged her on. I couldn't front, her antics were starting to get the best of me, and then Dalvin gave me a look, letting me know to chill.

"Fatima, you and your flock of chickens need to keep it movin'. I'm not in the mood for this."

"If you answer my question, I'll let you be."

"What question is that?" he replied, annoyance dripping from each word.

"Why haven't you called me? One minute we were cool, then the next, you got like Tom Cruise and became Mission Impossible."

Dalvin let out a long sigh and shook his head.

"I kicked it wit' you a couple of times on the humbug, and now you actin' like we had papers on each other. Step away from me wit' that nonsense. I'm with my people, and you disrespecting me, and you disrespecting her right now. And on the real, you one step from it being a major problem."

"What, is Mary Poppins over there supposed to be, your girl or something?"

"Yo, you already asked your one question."

"What is she gonna do for you? That little girl can't put it on you like a real woman can," Fatima remarked, with her hands on her wide hips and twisting her neck.

Once again, Dalvin eyed me and I remained quiet.

I quickly thought back to when I first met him during the parking space incident, and how I didn't understand why Demetrius remained mute, giving Dalvin control over the entire situation. But here I was, doing the exact same thing. Something about Dalvin just made you want to follow his lead.

"Now, what would you know about a real woman, Fatima?" he countered mockingly. "But just so you know, this is my girl, and she's holding it down like the classy young lady that she is."

All the color vanished from Fatima's face, and her friends were all shaking their heads, feeling embarrassed for their homegirl. But instead of Fatima bowing out with just an ounce of respect, she flipped out and reached over Dalvin trying to sneak in a sucker punch. But before her fist made contact with my face, Dalvin had his hand around her neck with her feet dangling in the air.

People started gathering around, but nobody dared to intervene. Fatima's own girlfriends had the look of fear in their eyes. A minute ago, they were carrying on and spitting jokes, but now they stood frozen.

I too was unable to move. Finally, I mustered the courage to speak. "Dalvin, let her go! You're gonna kill her!"

Fatima was gasping for air, and it was obvious that she couldn't breathe. But for a moment, it seemed that Dalvin was so caught up in what he was doing that he didn't hear what I said. Then he turned and looked at me and saw the horror in my eyes. At that moment, he dropped Fatima to the ground as if tossing a piece of trash.

Fatima was still gasping, trying to catch her breath. She was mortified at how Dalvin played her out, and she sat on the pavement, getting her bearings.

"Don't ever cross my path again. And if I even hear that you so much as spoke my girl's name, what just happened is nothing in comparison to what I will do to you. Are we clear?"

Fatima nodded her head, letting Dalvin know he made his point crystal clear. I swallowed hard, still trying to process what just happened.

"Are you okay?" he turned and asked as he stroked my cheek. I couldn't believe that one moment he seemed to be so cold, and in the very next moment, he was gentle and kind.

"I'm fine."

"So, are you gonna ride wit me or what?"

"Where we goin'?"

"You'll see. Y'all chill for a while. We 'bout to go somewhere for a few."

Keisha and Demetrius just nodded their heads yes. My eyes met with Keisha's, and it was clear that she was shaken up by what happened too; so shaken up, that for the first time in all the years I'd known her, she was speechless.

Dalvin put on NeYo's CD, and I sat back with my eyes closed, thinking as So Sick echoed out of his speakers.

For the entire sixteen years of my life, I had never witnessed any sort of violence. I mean, I had never even gotten into a fight before. Maybe I truly did live a sheltered life. But for some strange reason, Dalvin's behavior didn't bother me. I mean, seeing him flip on Fatima like that was a bit scary at first, but I knew he would never hurt me that way.

At the same time, it was wrong for Dalvin to put

his hands on a woman, but I reasoned that he was only protecting me. He was unlike any boy I had ever met, but yet, something about him reminded me so much of my dad. I adored my dad, but that same controlling behavior that I always detested from him was the same thing that was pulling my emotions even further into Dalvin.

"We're here."

When I opened my eyes, I couldn't believe where we were. "I haven't been here since I was a little girl. My dad used to take me here every weekend until he got too busy," I said, my voice trailing off as I reminisced about the past. We were at Grant Park, parked in front of the Buckingham Fountain.

"Whenever I got things on my mind, I come here. Somethin' about the water flowing just mellows me out," Dalvin explained.

"What do you have on your mind right now?"

"You. I can't get the look of fear I saw in your eyes when I had that minor altercation with Fatima out of my mind."

"If you think I'm scared of you, I'm not. I know you wouldn't hurt me. I can't lie, seeing you snatch that girl up like that did catch me off guard, but you were just protecting me, right?"

Dalvin gave me that million dollar smile as he rubbed his hand on the nape of my neck and played with my hair. "Yeah, I was protecting you, and also myself. I can't tolerate disrespect on any level. The second you let somethin' like that slide, everybody thinks they can try you."

"Did you mean what you said?"

"When I said what?"

"That I was your girl."

"I know I had no right to say that. I haven't even known you a week."

"I didn't mind. I wanted to be your girl the moment I laid eyes on you. I know you probably don't believe in love at first sight and think I'm corny, but it's true."

"Baby, you could never be corny. And I fell for you too. I mean I did give you my parking space, didn't I? You tried to act all tough, but you had the most angelic face I had ever seen." Dalvin leaned in and lightly kissed my lips.

He began pulling his head back, but I couldn't let him go. I put my hand on the back of his head and pulled him back in, my lips and tongue so desperately wanting to intertwine with his. I had kissed a couple of boys, but never did the firecrackers that were exploding in my heart happen before. His kiss told me that I held the key to his heart. I knew it was wrong and way too soon, but I wanted to go all the way with Dalvin, and couldn't stop myself from telling him.

"I want you to make love to me right now!" I whispered between kisses.

Dalvin immediately broke free from my embrace and just stared at me for a minute. "I know you not tryna give it up because of the whack garbage Fatima said."

"No, I just wanna be with you."

"Oh, so you want our first time to be right here in the car?"

"Does it really matter? I mean, if we feelin' each other does where we consummate our relationship make a difference?"

"That's how you gettin' down, just droppin' it for cats in their car?"

I felt the tears formulating in my eyes. I tried to hold

back, but I couldn't stop them from flowing. Dalvin had hurt my feelings so bad with that comment, that soon I was crying a river. "No, I'm not just givin' it up to guys! On the real, I'm still a virgin. I just wanna be with you in every way. Maybe what Fatima said did bother me, but I would've still wanted to be with you whether she said that or not."

"Don't cry. I'm sorry for hurting your feelings. You threw me off with what you said. I can't front, I want you too. I mean, bad, but not like this. I don't think you realize how special you are to me. I just want some more time to show you that before we take it there."

"I feel so embarrassed," I said, putting my head down.

Dalvin lifted my head back up. "Don't be. I'm flattered that you want me to be your first. But see, I want to be your first and your last."

With that, we fell into an intense, passionate kiss. Not only was I his girl, but I hoped one day, I'd be his wife.

Chapter 4

Truth Be Told

After the fiasco at the skating rink, Dalvin and I were inseparable. For the next few weeks, we would spend every free moment we had together. I actually had all the time in the world, and it was more so Dalvin making adjustments to his schedule in order to be with me.

My parents were oblivious to it all because Keisha was the perfect decoy. Every time I would go out, she'd be right by my side. Most of the time, she would chill with Demetrius while Dalvin and I would break out for some alone time. And on the few occasions that Demetrius was tied up handling business for Dalvin, I would let Keisha hold my car while I was with my man. Of course, she had no problem with that since she loved to floss in my whip.

One afternoon while Dalvin and I were having lunch at Heaven on Seven, I felt the urge to discuss something that had been on my mind. After taking the last bite of my chocolate pecan pie, I started sharing my thoughts.

"Baby, I'm tired of lying to my parents about where I be goin'. I think it's time I told them about you."

"I never told you to lie to your parents," Dalvin said nonchalantly while munching on his New Orleans BBQ shrimp.

"I know, but my dad is just so overprotective. I

wasn't sure how to tell him I have a boyfriend."

"It's simple. You say what you just told me."

"I'm serious, Dalvin."

"What you think, I'm playin'? I mean, Mercedes, you're sixteen years old, and in most states you're old enough to get married. I don't understand why you feel the need to lie."

"Well, have you told your parents about me?"

"No. But it's not because I'm afraid, and I definitely haven't lied to them."

"Then what is it? Are you ashamed of me?"

"Here we go! Shut up wit' that nonsense. I don't sit around havin' those types of conversations with my parents. I'ma do me regardless, so what I need to explain myself for? Plus, as long as I'm happy, then so is my father and mother."

I was listening to Dalvin, and although he was only a year older than me, it felt more like ten years. Why couldn't I have that type of relationship with my parents?

"So, would you like to meet my parents?" I asked, shyly.

"You think not? Without a doubt!"

"Seriously?"

"Of course! You're going to be my future wife."

I couldn't help but blush when Dalvin said that.

"So, when am I going to meet your parents?" I asked him.

"We can go now if you like."

"Not yet. First, I want you to meet my parents, and then I can meet yours."

"That works."

I felt so relieved after having my conversation with Dalvin. I was tired of lying to my parents, and I did want them to meet the guy that had my heart. It didn't make any sense to keep this charade going.

After lunch, Dalvin and I kissed each other goodbye and went our separate ways. He had work he needed to handle for his dad, and I was actually anxious to get home and tell my parents about him.

Keisha picked me up, and I had to share my news with her. "Girl, I had a long talk with Dalvin, and I'm going to introduce him to my parents."

"What?" Keisha squealed, not surprisingly shocked by my announcement.

"Yeah, this sneaking around has to stop. I mean, I'm not a little girl anymore. It's time that my parents accept that I'm growing up."

"You mean your dad, 'cause I doubt Auntie Toy will have a problem with it."

"The main obstacle will be my dad, but I have a good feelin' that he'll really like Dalvin. They kinda remind me of each other in a lot of ways."

"You mean they both got that calm, cool, controlling aura about them," Keisha stated matter of factly.

"No doubt."

"Did you ever ask Dalvin what his father does? He gets all that bravado from somewhere."

"Not yet. It seems like every time I'm 'bout to, we get caught up in somethin' else."

"I bet, like kissin' and lickin' and all that good stuff. I know he be puttin' it down. He looks like he got mad skills."

"Keisha, you need to stop. But truth be told, we haven't even gone all the way yet."

"Excuse me?"

"I'm serious. Dalvin wants to wait. I tried a couple

of times, but he wasn't havin' it."

"See, that's the control freak in him. He wants to be the one to decide when y'all make love for the first time."

"I know, right! I hope he hurries up, 'cause I'm dyin' for him to pop my cherry."

"Darn, Mercedes! I be forgettin' you still ain't taken a bite from the apple. But once you do, it's all she wrote. I know for a long time I was all hung up on my first. After we broke up, I basically became a stalker."

I burst out laughing listening to Keisha's story.

"Laugh if you want, but I'm serious. It got so bad that he threatened to have his sister beat me up if I didn't stop harassin' him."

"He didn't have to call big sis on you? What happened? Why y'all break up?"

"Girl, I was fourteen and he was sixteen, and poppin' cherries was his specialty. I was just another neighborhood conquest to him. I can't front, that dude crushed me, but eventually I took it as one to grow on."

"Dang, man! I hope Dalvin don't do that to me after we make love."

"Naw, Dalvin's really feelin' you, I can tell. Y'all be walkin' around like two lovebirds."

"I do love him. That's why I'm hoping that my dad will accept him, because they're the two most important men in my life."

When we pulled up to my house, my stomach started getting butterflies. There was no way I was changing my mind, and I was praying it would all go smoothly. I had been practicing in my mind how the script would go, but everything was easier when you were just rehearsing.

When we got inside the house, Keisha and I headed upstairs because I wanted to go to the bathroom before I had my encounter with my parents.

Before I could make the first step, I heard my mother call out for me. Keisha and I walked back towards the den where we heard my mother's voice coming from.

"Ma, did you call me?"

"Yes, I did. Keisha, you can go upstairs. I need to speak to Mercedes alone."

Keisha and I looked at each other, because it definitely sounded like my mom had beef with me, but about what, I had no clue. Keisha did as my mother said and headed upstairs, or knowing her, she was lurking somewhere in the corner trying to get an earful.

"What's goin' on, Ma? You sound real serious."

"I wanna discuss somethin' with you."

"That's cool, because I wanted to talk to you about somethin' too."

"I'm goin' first.

"Okay."

"Today I was driving down Michigan Avenue and I saw you and some boy coming out a restaurant holding hands and kissing. What's that about, Mercedes?"

"I can explain."

"You betta, 'cause when I tell your Daddy, he gon' flip out and take away that convertible, and you gon' be stuck in this here house."

"Ma, just calm down. I was plannin' on tellin' you about Dalvin."

"Oh, that's his name?"

"Yes, he's my boyfriend, and we're in love."

My mother stood, shaking her head for a minute.

"Truth be told, when I came home today, I planned on tellin' you and Daddy about him, but you found out before I had a chance. But, Ma, please don't tell Daddy.

Let me bring Dalvin home so y'all can meet him."

"Mercedes, how long you been seeing this boy?"

"Since the day after I got home."

"That's over a month! You been lying to me and your Daddy 'bout where you been goin' all this time!"

"I know, Ma, and I'm not proud of that, but you know how Daddy is. I just didn't know how to tell him. But I'm sixteen now. You had me at fifteen. Isn't it time I was able to have a boyfriend?"

"The point is, you've been lying, Mercedes. How are we supposed to trust you?"

"I was plannin' on telling you the truth. I'm serious, you have to believe me. If anybody should understand, it's you, Ma."

I watched my mother sip on her drink and dangle her shoe off her foot. As I stared at her, I actually felt sorry for my mother. There she sat, still so young and beautiful, but she was almost like a caged bird. For most of her life, she had me to fuss over and keep her busy. But after I went off to boarding school and started growing up, it's like she lost her favorite doll to play with. She didn't have any girlfriends, and the same way my dad tried to control me, he did the same to her. I doubted my mother was even upset that I had a boyfriend. She was probably concerned about how my dad would react.

"Alright, Mercedes, I won't say nothin' to your Dad, but we need to meet your boyfriend immediately. Tomorrow wouldn't be too soon."

"Thanks, Ma. I'm on it. I just know you'll love him." I gave my mom a hug and a kiss and headed upstairs. Of course, as I expected, Keisha was lurking in the corner.

"Girl, I can't believe Aunt Toy busted you."

"Who you tellin'? I'm just glad she didn't flip out

too much."

"Yeah, she handled it well. It was probably the way you played on her soft spot. You betta hope you're as lucky with Uncle Ronny."

"Now, all I have to do is call Dalvin and see how soon he can meet my parents."

"Girl, I can't wait to be a fly on the wall for this one."

Later on, I called Dalvin. He was looking forward to meeting my parents, and he had no problem coming over the next day. I was happy that he was so positive, because although I was excited about introducing him to my parents, I wasn't able to sleep that night. I tossed and turned all night. I didn't even tell my father I was bringing my boyfriend home. I decided to just surprise him. I knew that every Wednesday afternoon he handled some business in his office, so he would be home.

The next morning when I woke up, I took a quick shower, dressed and headed out. I was meeting Dalvin for breakfast because I wanted to talk to him before he came over later that afternoon.

When I pulled up to the Original Pancake House, Dalvin's Range Rover was already parked. I went inside and he was sitting in a booth. "Hi, baby."

"What's up?" he said, and gave me a kiss. "I already ordered our food."

"Thanks. I'm so glad you were able to meet me this morning. I definitely wanted to see you before you came over later."

"You need to calm down, it's not that deep. Your parents will love me, trust me."

"You're always so confident."

"Yeah, I'm hoping a little will rub off on you. But just in case it doesn't, this should help." Dalvin pulled out an Elara jewelry box. "Open it."

It took me a moment to get past my disbelief. I finally opened the box, and the most beautiful three stoned horizontal diamond necklace was sparkling in my face. "Dalvin, it's gorgeous!"

"I thought so too. The diamonds are flawless, just like you. When you're wearing that necklace, it should give you all the confidence in the world, and never let you doubt how much I love you."

"I love you too."

"After I meet your parents, I made reservations for us at this exclusive restaurant, and I got us a suite at the Chicago Drake Hotel."

"Does that mean what I think it means?" I asked cautiously before gettin' too excited.

Dalvin grabbed my hand and interlaced his fingers through mine while gazing into my eyes lovingly. "If you're ready, I think it's time we take our relationship to the next level."

"I been ready. I was waiting for you."

"That's what I wanted to hear."

Dalvin leaned over the table and we tasted each other's lips. All I could say to myself was, Dang, I'm in love!

After our food came, we ate and talked some more. Then Dalvin went to handle some business for his father. and I headed home to prepare for my Meet the Parents afternoon.

I decided that during our dinner later on tonight, I would finally remember to ask Dalvin exactly what type of business his father owned. I mean, if I was going to be his wife, it was only right that I knew what type of empire my husband would be running someday.

When I returned home, my father was locked in his office, and my mother and Keisha were eating at the kitchen table.

"Good morning, ladies!" I said, cheerfully.

"Aren't you in a good mood!" my mother said.

"So you noticed."

"It's hard not to. Your whole face is beaming," Keisha pointed out.

"Yes, it's the face of a young woman in love," I said.

"I remember when I was your age and your Daddy had me feeling the exact same way," my mother said, reflecting on her younger days.

"Aunt Toy, you still be havin' that love struck look on your face when you around Uncle Ronny."

"I know, but there's nothin' like feeling it for the very first time. I'm happy for you, Mercedes."

"You mean that, Ma?"

"Of course I do. I just hope this young man that's stolen my little girl's heart is worthy."

"He is, Ma. Here, look at this necklace he gave me this morning when we met for breakfast."

"So that's where you snuck off all early!" Keisha said, rolling her eyes.

"I wanted to see him before he came over to meet you guys."

By this time, my mother and Keisha were inspecting the sparkler around my neck."

"Wow, this is hot, Mercedes."

"Thank you, Keisha."

"It is beautiful. This boy must be really smitten with you. What does he do for a living to be able to afford somethin' so pricey?"

"He works for his father in the family business."

"What business is that?"

"I don't know. We haven't had a chance to talk about that yet."

"Yeah, they be too busy kissin' and stuff, Auntie Toy."

"Hum, I bet they do. I hope you're being careful, young lady. Your Daddy would go on a rampage if you walked up in this house pregnant."

"Ma, we're not even havin' sex."

"Not yet, but all it takes is one time."

"Is that what happened with you and Daddy? That first time, did you all conceive me?"

"That was a different time. I knew your father was going to be the man I would spend the rest of my life with. Please, that man saved me. I was stuck in the projects of Harlem, going nowhere. Your Daddy was the answer to all my prayers. Without him, I don't know what would've come of me."

"But, Ma, you're so beautiful; you could've been anything you wanted to be."

"You're so naive, Mercedes. All that beauty was gettin' me nowhere. It just made me a target for all the thirsty, grimy men out there preying on young women. I was hardly educated because I was too busy working, tryna bring home some extra money for my mother. I didn't have no life, and to me, my future was dim."

"So, how did you meet Uncle Ronny?" Keisha asked.

"One afternoon, as I was walking home from my job at the neighborhood cleaners, this big, black spankin' new Mercedes pulled up next to me. My eyes got so big, 'cause I hadn't neva seen no car like that up close before. I just knew it was probably some old white nasty man inside trying to pick me up, but when he rolled down the window and I saw that man staring back at me, my heart started beating real fast. O-o-o w-e-e-e was your Daddy fine! I couldn't believe he was interested in me."

"Why you say that? I saw your pictures when you were my age, and you were beautiful."

"You saw me when your Daddy had cleaned me up. I was what you call a diamond in the serious rough when he met me. I never put no time into my looks, because I was afraid the prettier I looked, the more unwanted attention I would draw to myself. The last thing I wanted to be bothered with was those trifling men in my neighborhood, but your Daddy was able to see beyond all that."

"So what did he say to you, Auntie Toy?"

"He said, 'You need a ride home? It's too hot for you to be walking home.' Although I was dying to get in that air conditioned luxury car, I told him I had two good feet that would get me home just fine. So for the next ten minutes, he drove slowly and followed me home."

"What?" Keisha and I said in unison.

"Yep, he sure did. For the next week, everyday I got off of work, he would be parked right outside waiting for me, and he'd follow me home until finally I did get in that car with him. And I've been riding with him ever since."

"That's so romantic, Ma."

"I think so too. That's why I named you Mercedes. Meeting your Daddy that day in his car was the best gift I had ever received, until I had you. I thought it was only right I give you that name."

"I hope Dalvin and I have what you and Daddy have one day."

"You really care about him that deeply?"

"I do. I mean, if I could, I'd spend the rest of my life

with him. I can't imagine meeting anyone else that would make me happier."

I wanted today to be the beginning of Dalvin and me spending the rest of our lives together. If my dad could accept him as my boyfriend, I knew our relationship would just blossom. There would be no more sneaking around or hiding our love. We could do family dinners with his parents and my parents. Maybe my mother and Dalvin's mother could go shopping together, get their hair and nails done together, and my mom could finally have a female friend to hang out with. I prayed that my every wish would come true.

Chapter 5

Dangerously In Love

"Girl, you betta hurry up! Dalvin will be here any minute," Keisha reminded me.

"Time flies so fast. I can't believe its two o'clock already. How do I look?" I asked Keisha, turning around to face her.

"Very cute and innocent. I assume that's the look you goin' for."

"Exactly! My dad picked out this outfit for me."

I studied myself one more time in the full-length mirror. The soft pink Capri pants with a matching ruffled twin shirt had angelic schoolgirl written all over it. The finishing touch was the "token of love" necklace Dalvin gave me. He was right. Having it on gave me a definite sense of confidence.

Just as Keisha and I reached the bottom of the stairs, we heard the doorbell.

"Girl, he's right on time. D must really be in love wit' you, 'cause men are always late."

I couldn't help but smile, because I loved Dalvin just as much. I knew our maid, Lillian had probably gotten the front door. I walked around and saw that my dad's office door was still closed. My mother was in the den flipping through her fashion magazines, so I ran to the front door to greet Dalvin.

"I got this, Lillian. Thanks so much." As she walked away, I gave Dalvin a big hug and kiss. Feeling his strong arms around me, I knew everything would go great.

"Baby, you smell good, and you look good too. Although your outfit is a bit on the preppy side."

"You don't like it?"

"I like whatever you wear. So, where's the family?"

"I'm glad you're so anxious."

"Why wouldn't I be? So, show me the way."

"First, I'm going to introduce you to my mother. She's the soft one. Then, I'll have her go get my dad, because he's been stuck in his office all day working."

"Whatever works for you, baby."

I led Dalvin to the den where Keisha was now sitting with my mother. They both looked up at the same time when we walked in the room.

"Hi, D," Keisha said, waving her hand.

"Hello," he responded.

"So, you must be the young man Mercedes has been raving about. It's a pleasure to meet you."

"Thank you, Mrs. Clinton. It's a pleasure to meet you too. You have a beautiful home. Mercedes, you and your Mother look just alike," Dalvin said, smiling at me.

"Well, come have a seat and get comfortable. Would you like Lillian to bring you something to drink or anything?"

"No, I'm fine, but thank you."

"So, how old are you, Dalvin?"

"Seventeen."

"Oh, so you have one more year left in high school?"

"Actually, I graduated this year."

"So, what are your plans?"

"I'm attending DePaul University while I continue to work with my father in the family business."

"That's impressive."

"And of course, in between that, whenever Mercedes has time for me, I'll be with her."

I squeezed Dalvin's hand as I listened to him win my mother over. I could tell that she had genuinely taken a liking to him."

"Mercedes, I'll go get your Dad so he can meet Dalvin."

"A'ight, one down, one to go. Auntie Toy seemed like she was feeling you, D," Keisha said.

Dalvin and I continued to hold hands, waiting for my mother to come back with my dad. I was feeling extremely optimistic, especially since my mom obviously was digging him.

When they finally walked in, I could tell my mom had given my dad a pep talk and filled him in. Luckily, my dad didn't appear to be upset, which was a good sign.

"Hi, Daddy," I said, standing up, with a wide grin spread across my face. I let go of Dalvin's hand and walked towards my dad. I gave him a hug and he kissed me on my forehead.

"Baby girl, your mother tells me you have a friend you'd like me to meet."

"Yes, Daddy, I do."

Dalvin stood up and turned around to face my dad. "How you doing, sir?" Dalvin said, as he walked towards my dad, extending his arm so he could shake his hand.

I was watching Dalvin as he came towards us, and when I turned back to look at my dad, he had the strangest look on his face. The smiles that were on me, Keisha's and my mom's faces all started to fade as we studied the negative energy my dad was giving off.

"Daddy, this is Dalvin," I stated, still not giving up the hope that all was well.

"Your father is Dalvin Dewitt," Daddy stated, as if he knew this for a fact.

Dalvin eyed him suspiciously before speaking. "As a matter of fact, he is. Do you know my father?"

"Yes, very well."

"That's great, Daddy! You guys do business together." My voice sounded chipper and upbeat, but I knew my dad all too well, and for whatever reason, he wasn't happy to see my boyfriend.

"I'm Ronald Clinton, but then you should know that."

"Actually, Mercedes never told me your name, but of course, who hasn't heard of the great Ronald Clinton. It's an honor to meet you."

Dalvin kept his hand extended, but Daddy refused to shake it. He just continued to eye Dalvin in a vile way.

"Latoya, go get Lillian and have her show Mr. Dewitt the front door."

Like the dutiful wife, my mother turned to get Lillian without asking any questions.

"Ma, wait a minute!"

She turned to me with that same pathetic look she got in her eyes whenever she thought a confrontation would ensue between her and my dad. "Daddy, what are you doing? Dalvin just got here and I wanted you to meet him."

"I did meet him, and now it's time for him to go," he answered defiantly.

"I'm not ready for him to go. Dalvin is my boyfriend,

Daddy. I want you to be respectful towards him."

"I see. First, he's your friend, now he's been upgraded to boyfriend. It don't make a difference, because I don't ever want you to see this boy again. Do you understand? Now, I mean what I say."

"Daddy, what are you sayin'?" I questioned, with my voice rising.

"It's okay, Mercedes, I'll leave. We can talk about this later."

"You must've not understood me. There will be no talking later today, or any other day. I forbid you to ever see my daughter again."

"No disrespect, Mr. Clinton, but you can't forbid me to do anything."

"I think everybody should calm down," my mom said, feeling the tension in the room. "I think you should leave, Dalvin."

"No, he shouldn't. He's my guest. Why are you treating him this way, Daddy?"

"We can discuss this later. Right now, I want this boy out of my house."

Dalvin stared at my dad with the same glare he had on Fatima that night. My hands started shaking because I didn't want the two men in my life to go to blows. I tried to figure out what I missed, and why this was happening to me. "If Dalvin is leaving, then so am I."

I heard Keisha let out a deep sigh. She put her hand over her mouth and began shaking her head.

"Mercedes, you don't want to do that," my mother calmly spoke, trying to be the voice of reason.

"Your mother's right. You stay here. We'll talk later." Then Dalvin turned to my dad. "I think there are some things your father would like to discuss with you."

He followed my mother out, and I was livid with my dad.

"How dare you treat someone that I care about like that! Daddy, I never thought I would be ashamed of you, but your behavior was horrible. Dalvin has never done anything to you."

"Baby girl, I know you're upset, so I'm gonna let this disrespect slide."

"I don't want to let it slide. I want to know why you treated my boyfriend like that."

"First of all, that's not your boyfriend. And I'm in no mood to discuss my decisions with you. You're my daughter. You answer my questions, not the other way around."

"How dare you!" My voice was now quivering due to my anger. "I love him! You will explain yourself to me!"

"You what? I know you're not havin' scx with that boy!" he yelled.

"That's none of your business!"

"Mercedes, that's enough!" my mom shrieked.

My dad then grabbed my arm and held it tightly. "You answer me! Are you sleeping with that boy?"

"Let me go!" I hollered rebelliously.

"No, she's not, Uncle Ronny." Keisha had never seen my dad put his hands on me, or me raise my voice at him. I'm sure the entire episode was freaking her out. But I didn't care. I needed answers. My dad had to explain to me why he detested Dalvin so much without even giving him a chance. It was clear it had something to do with Dalvin's father, but why should my boyfriend be held responsible because of something going on between him and his dad?

After Keisha said her peace, my dad unlocked me

from his grip. It didn't matter, because I still wanted answers.

"Mercedes, you've never defied me before, and don't start now. If I'm telling you not to do somethin', it's for your own good. All you need to know is that boy's father is my enemy, which means he's an enemy to this entire family, including you." With that, my dad stormed off, leaving me standing there with even more questions than answers. My mom followed behind him like the good wife. At that moment, they both disgusted me.

"Girl, I can't believe you spoke to Uncle Ronny like that! You done lost your mind!"

"My mind? Look how he treated Dalvin, the guy that I love."

"Mercedes, I understand that, but you know how your dad is. But on the real, D's people must be official, because he didn't flinch when your dad came at him all sideways. He was just as cool and confident as he always is."

"What's your point, Keisha?"

"My point is, that you ain't dealin' wit' no buster. Whatever family business Dalvin's in, it's some next level stuff. I mean, your daddy said they were his enemy. Who got enough paper and power to ruffle your pop's feathers?"

Keisha did have a point, but all this did was make me more curious as to what my dad did for a living. I mean, he's throwing words around like "enemy". Those are fighting words.

Later on that night when everybody was sleep, I called Dalvin from my cell phone. "Hi, baby. I'm sorry about how my dad treated you earlier today."

"Don't worry about it. It's not your fault."

"I still want to see you tonight."

"I wanna see you too. Can you get out?"

"Yeah, I think so. But can you come get me? If someone notices my car missing, there could be a problem."

"Alright, so meet me at the corner down from your house in a half."

"Okay. I love you."

"Love you too." I looked over and was glad that Keisha was in a coma.

I tiptoed to the bathroom so I could freshen up. I put on a cotton baby doll dress and some flip-flops. I grabbed my purse, cell and went downstairs to sneak out. Luckily, I still remembered the code to the alarm and disarmed it so I could leave without waking the whole house up. By the time I made it down the hill and to the corner, I saw Dalvin waiting right on time. I got in the car and he drove off.

"Baby, you know one of the things that I love about you?" I asked.

"What's that?"

"You're always so punctual."

"Gotta be. My Father always told me that for every second you're late, somebody's waiting to take your place. I can't afford to take those types of risks."

"I want you to be honest with me."

"Always am."

"What family business are you in?"

Dalvin turned down the music and glanced at me. Then he turned back and kept his eyes on the road. "Are you gon' ride wit' me?"

"What do you mean?"

"I mean, are you gon' ride this thing out wit' me.

Hold me down, stay by my side no matter what. Be a soldier."

I didn't quite understand what he meant, but I knew I loved him and that was enough. "Baby, yes I'ma ride it all the way out with you."

"Remember you said that."

"I mean it. So, now will you answer my question?"

"My father runs half the streets of Chicago and just about every other part of Illinois. He's into everything, from weapons, narcotics, money laundering… you name it, he's got his hands in it. And the half my father don't run, your father does," Dalvin stated point blank.

"My dad is a criminal?" I asked, sounding more hurt than surprised.

"Yeah, and so am I. Can you handle that?"

My mouth remained open as I digested what Dalvin told me. I started replaying the last sixteen years of my life—or at least the years I could remember. All the fancy cars, the many mansions and vacation homes we had. The endless shopping sprees, and the tons of jewelry and furs my mother owned. The sky-high tuition for private schools and extravagant birthday parties I was accustomed to. My life seemed to be like no others. No, my dad wasn't a famous movie star, a superstar athlete, or a Wall Street mogul that I read about in Time magazine. But yet, I never gave much thought to where all the millions and millions of dollars came from, or how we were able to live the lifestyle of some of the most successful people in the United States.

The only thing that kept playing in my mind was when I was six years old and my dad said, "Mo' money, mo' problems."

"Mercedes, are you going to answer me, or what?"

"Did you know who I was when you met me? I have to know."

"Of course not. If I did, I would've spoken on it. I mean, Clinton is a fairly common last name. Now I'm not gone front, when I pulled up to your crib, I started havin' my suspicions. Not many brothers in Chicago are livin' like that, unless your name is Michael Jordan or Oprah Winfrey. But by then, it was too late. Plus, I was hopin' I was wrong."

"So, why do your father and my dad got so much beef?"

"On the real, my pops and your pops was crazy cool at one time. Then a few years ago, their business relationship just started deteriorating. It's like they didn't want to play together no more. I don't know if it was greed or what. My father honestly never spoke about it too much with me. It seemed like it fell apart overnight. Once a week, all the heads of each family meets for a meeting, and one day I overheard my father saying your dad would no longer be attending the meetings."

How did my dad know who you were?"

"I have no idea, because I don't ever remember meeting him before. But then again, I'm the spitting image of my dad, so it's not hard to tell. It's crazy, because I had no idea your father even had a daughter."

"I guess with the business he's in, I'm one of his best kept secrets. Maybe that's why he was so adamant about me goin' away to a boarding school. He didn't want me to find out about his illegal business activities."

"Or maybe he was just protecting you. It's different when you have a daughter."

"Whatever! But it still doesn't give him the right to forbid me from seeing you. The issues that he has are with your father, not you."

"In his mind, my father and I are one in the same."

"So, how do you feel?"

"Honestly, I can understand your father's point of view, but at the same time, I'm in love with you, and I don't want anything or anyone to come between us."

"How do you think your parents would feel if they knew we were together?"

"Like I told you before, my parents just want me to be happy. But I do know my father will ask me if you'll be loyal to me if you ever had to make a choice."

"You mean between you and my dad?"

"Yes, because although I would never ask you to choose, I'm sure your dad will. Because, let's be clear, Mercedes, I'm a man, and I won't sneak or hide my relationship with you for nobody, and that includes your father. So, if you gon' be wit' me, then I'ma claim what's mine."

I thought about what Dalvin said, and I did want to be loyal to him. I deserved to be happy, and he truly made me happy.

When we arrived at the hotel suite, it was decorated with flowers, candles and a bottle of champagne was sitting in an ice bucket.

"You did all this for me? How did you know I was still coming?"

"I wasn't sure, but I never stopped hoping. Here, put this on," he said, handing me a bag from Neiman Marcus.

"Okay, I'll be right back."

When I got into the bathroom, I was so nervous— not in a bad way, but anxious. I took the box out of the bag and opened it. There was a beautiful white silk Georgette halter lingerie ensemble. Before putting it on, I took a shower and then lathered my body with some of the hotel's lotion. After slipping on the lingerie, I opened the door, and Dalvin had lit all the candles and scattered rose pedals from the bathroom leading to the bed. My feet felt like they were floating as I made my way towards him. He was sitting on the edge of the king-sized bed with only his silk boxer shorts on. The luminous light seemed to highlight every muscle in his arms, chest and abs.

"I poured you a glass of champagne, although I'm not even sure you drink."

"I'm a virgin, Dalvin, not a saint." We both laughed.

"Let's make a toast." He handed me my champagne and we held up our glasses. "To our love, and nothing coming between it. And to no matter what, you'll ride wit' me."

"Of course I will. But baby, not to ruin the mood, I hope you brought protection. I would hate to get pregnant. I know neither one of us is ready for a baby."

"I got you," Dalvin said, caressing the side of my cheek. I do hope one day you are the mother of my child but I know right now neither one of us is ready to be parents."

I couldn't help but blush at knowing that in the future, Dalvin hoped I would be the woman who would carry his child. We then clinked our glasses, and by the time I had my last swallow, I was dying to have Dalvin inside of me. He laid me down on the bed and hypnotized me with his eyes before tenderly sprinkling my body with kisses. My back arched as he made his way further down my stomach. He paused for a moment.

"Baby, don't stop! You feel so good!"

He continued until he reached the gates to heaven. With the first stroke of his tongue, my entire body shivered. He continued, leaving me yearning for more. While I was trying to catch my breath, in the typical smooth way he did everything, I noticed Dalvin slip on a condom. Before I knew it, I felt the tip of his head gently making its way inside me. I moaned in pain, but it was an intoxicating pain.

"Mercedes, am I hurting you? Do you want me to stop?"

"No, please don't!"

Dalvin continued as I grasped my nails tightly into his back and buried my face in his chest, getting through the pain of him popping my cherry. "Oh, Mercedes!" he moaned, as he went further inside of me.

Although I didn't think it was possible, at that moment I fell even deeper in love with him. He rocked inside of me, and we kissed fervently for what seemed like a lifetime.

Eventually, we fell asleep in each other's arms, and I wished that night could've lasted forever.

Chapter 6

Family Affair

When I finally woke up the next day, to my horror, it was almost twelve in the afternoon. I looked around for Dalvin, and realized he was in the bathroom taking a shower. I jumped out of bed and grabbed my purse to retrieve my cell phone. Last night was the most memorable experience of my life, but the thought of getting caught was so petrifying that I couldn't even enjoy it. I saw three missed calls from Keisha. I immediately called her back, hoping to find out if my cover had been blown.

"Girl, where you at?" was the greeting I received from my cousin.

"Do my parents know I didn't come home last night?"

"Not yet, but I don't know how much longer I can tell your mother you're still sleep. She wanted to come up here and check on you three times already, but I told her you was crying half the night and finally went to sleep early this morning."

"Thanks for the cover story. What about my dad? Where's he?"

"He had some business to take care of early this morning and hasn't been back since. I'm glad you didn't drive your car. That was the one smart thing you did. But you shoulda told me you was sneaking out, instead of havin' me figure this mess out on my own. I figured you had run off with D. I hope you plan on comin' back though."

"No doubt. Listen, keep my moms from comin' upstairs. I'm goin' to call you when Dalvin drops me off at the corner from my house. Then you fake like I just left the house and went for a walk. Tell her I was still upset and wanted to be alone, alright?"

"I got you, but hurry up. We don't need no more drama up in here."

Right when I hung the phone up, Dalvin stepped out of the bathroom. He was all wet and looking too sexy. "Who was you on the phone wit'?"

"Keisha. I didn't realize how late it was. She called me a couple of times, and I wanted to make sure my cover hadn't been blown."

"I told you I wasn't gonna be sneakin' around wit' you. I'm not hiding our relationship."

"I understand that, Dalvin. But at the same time, I have to find a way to try to mend things with my family. I'm hopin' to soften my mother up so she can convince my dad that he shouldn't try to keep us apart."

"You handle your situation how you see fit, but it's about us now. After last night, you're mine, and there's no turning back."

"I don't wanna turn back. This is where I wanna be."

Before I could say another word, Dalvin and I were making love, and I forgot all about going home.

By the time I had showered and dressed, another hour had passed and I was fidgeting the whole time Dalvin was driving me home. I knew ending my relationship with him was out of the question, but I also didn't want any beef at home. What was once a beautiful thing was quickly turning into a complicated nightmare.

"What are you doin'?" I asked, caught off guard by where Dalvin was going.

"Taking you home."

"You can't drive up to the front of my house."

"What, you want me to drop you back off at the corner like you some 'hood rat?"

"Dalvin, stop it!"

"Stop what? Is that what you tellin' me to do?"

"When you picked me up from the corner last night was I a 'hood rat?"

"That was different, and today is a new day. I'm not dropping no girl of mine at some corner like we ashamed of what we have."

"I'm beggin' you to please stop the car and don't go up that driveway! You know I'm not ashamed of you, but at the same time, I can't just spit in my parents' faces and let them know I stayed out all night with you after what went down yesterday. If they find out now, there's no telling what my dad might do."

Dalvin backed his truck up and turned around, going back towards the corner. A sense of relief came over me.

"Baby, I know you didn't want to do that, but thank you. What we shared was so beautiful. I don't want to ruin that with an argument. I love you so much, and I'll fix this with my parents."

"I hope you're right, Mercedes, because I'm not gonna lose you."

"No, you're not, I promise you that." I leaned over and kissed him, sensing his anger towards me. "I have to go, but I'll call you as soon as I get a free moment."

I blew him a kiss goodbye, and he drove off without even saying a word to me. I was devastated by how he reacted, because I didn't understand what he expected me to do. I did love him and wanted to be with him, but I loved my family too.

"This has to be, Keisha," I said out loud as the sound of my cell phone ringing interrupted my thoughts.

"Girl, where you at?" Keisha belted, sounding like the heat was on.

"I'm at the corner. You can go 'head and tell my moms that I went for a walk."

"A'ight, but I'ma tell her that you seemed really upset, so I'ma head out to make sure you're okay."

"Cool, so I'll be waiting for you at the corner."

A few minutes later, Keisha came jogging down the hill towards me.

"How did it go?"

"Good. She don't know anythin' is up."

"Thank goodness!" I gave Keisha a hug, "Girl, I owe you big time."

"You best believe. I know exactly how you can pay me back too. I saw these cute jeans in your closet that I'm dying to squeeze my butt into."

"Don't nothin' change with you. But you earned them, so you can have 'em."

"Auntie Toy is feelin' real bad about how everything went down yesterday. She can tell you're really digging D, and she thought he seemed like a cool dude."

"But of course she's on my dad's side, not wanting to cause no waves."

"Well, yeah, but I can tell it's weighing heavy on her mind. I think if you play your cards right, you might be able to break her."

"Word?"

"It's no guarantee, but when I told her you was

crying and how you went for a walk and didn't want to be bothered, it hurt her to her heart. She does want you to be happy. All she kept sayin' was that it was just your luck that your boyfriend would have to be the son of Uncle Ronny's enemy."

"Who you tellin'? I'm still tryna figure that one out."

"All that is cool, but I want the real 411. What happened wit' you and D?"

"I'm happy to announce that I'm no longer as pure as the driven snow."

Keisha started jumping up and down in the middle of the street. Luckily we lived on a cul-de-sac, so hardly any cars came down our street. "I knew it! That's why you're glowing! Girl, I want all the details."

I broke down how everything went down, piece by piece for her. Replaying it made me want to pick up the phone and call Dalvin right there on the spot.

"That sounds incredible, Mercedes. No wonder it took you so long to get home."

"Last night and this morning was magical, but by the time Dalvin dropped me off, he left without saying two words to me."

"Why?"

"He wanted to drop me off at my front door, and of course I couldn't let that go down. I tried to explain to him that I needed time to bring my parents around to accepting him, but he didn't care. I mean after the way my dad treated him, I don't blame him, but still, that's my dad."

"He'll come around, Mercedes."

"Who, my dad or Dalvin?"

"Hopefully both, but definitely D. You guys share a deep bond now, and that's not gonna be easy to break."

"But you shoulda seen his face when he left, Keisha. It was like I had disappointed him. I don't know how I'ma make this right. If I can't get my dad to come around, what am I gonna do? I love Dalvin so much, I can't let him go."

"You have to find a way to make Uncle Ronny see that without him feeling as if you're choosing Dalvin over him. Did you find out why they have so much beef?"

"Yes, but you have to swear to secrecy not to say anything."

"We family, you know it's not leaving this right here," Keisha stated as she pointed her finger down to the space between us.

"Dalvin's father is a crime lord, and runs half of the streets of Chicago. And guess who runs the other half?"

"Uncle Ronny?"

"Bingo!"

"I knew Dalvin's family was official. That cat just had too much swagger wit him."

"Forget about that. What about my dad being a criminal?"

"Mercedes, you tellin' me you had no idea that your dad was the man on the streets?'

"No. Did you?"

"Pretty much. I mean, I would listen to little comments my moms would make about Uncle Ronny, and then look at how your living. Dude, come on now. I've watched plenty episodes of Cribs on MTV, and don't none of them houses come close to that mansion sitting on top of that hill. So somethin' had to give."

"Yeah, maybe I just didn't want to face the truth. But now I have no choice."

"I'ma start callin' you the 'Black Mafia Princess'. No

matter which direction you go in, it's gangsta either way."

Keisha and I stayed outside for another fifteen minutes before heading back to the house. As soon as we walked in, we noticed my mother sitting at the bottom of the wraparound stairs. "I've been waiting for you, Mercedes."

"Ma, I'm really not in the mood to talk."

"Well, then can you just listen?"

"Go 'head."

"Mercedes, I know you're furious with your father, and probably me too, but we're family, and we're gonna get past this."

"I don't see that happenin' as long as Daddy won't let me see Dalvin."

"You have to understand that in your father's business, he has to be careful, and you dating the son of his enemy can cause a lot of problems."

"You mean illegal problems?"

"I didn't say that."

"You didn't have to. It's pretty obvious that Daddy is involved in criminal activities, and because of that, I'm being punished."

"Your father isn't tryna punish you."

"Well, he is if he doesn't allow me to see Dalvin. Ma, I don't think you understand. I'm in love with Dalvin. I want to spend the rest of my life with him. I want him to be the father of my children."

"You had sex with him, didn't you?" she asked in a solemn tone.

"I never said that."

"It's in your eyes… your voice. When did you have sex with him? Did you see him last night? Answer me, Mercedes!" my mother demanded to know.

I began walking away, but she yanked my arm, pulling me back. "You answer me!"

"Yes, I did see him last night, and yes, we made love."

Before I could blink, I felt the sting of my mom's hand as she slapped me. "How dare you be disloyal to this family! I was racking my brain tryna figure out how to make this right, feeling torn between your happiness and pleasing your father, and having a guilty conscience because my little girl was so hurt. But instead of crying yourself to sleep, you was out sleeping wit the enemy!"

"Dalvin isn't the enemy!" I roared. "You don't ever defend me when it comes to Daddy. All you do is bow down to him like he's God, even when he's wrong, and I'm sick of it. He has no right to keep me from Dalvin, and you know it. I don't care that my father saved you from your so-called misery. I deserve to be happy, and I won't let you or anybody else keep me from that!" I stormed off upstairs and locked my bedroom door. I didn't care anymore. Enough was enough. I wanted to be with Dalvin, and I refused to let anybody destroy our love.

For the next couple of hours, first Keisha, then my mother, and finally my dad knocked on my bedroom door, wanting to discuss the blowup I had with my mother. But I refused to unlock my door, because to me, there was nothing to discuss.

The only person I wanted to talk to was Dalvin, and his phone had been going straight to voice mail. I'd already left him three messages, and I was becoming impatient waiting for him to call me back.

Becoming restless, I started listening to NeYo's, Let Go. I decided to put it on repeat, and eventually fell into a deep sleep.

When I finally woke up, I realized I had been in a

coma for over five hours. It was now after nine, and I was starving. I looked at my cell phone, and I had no messages or missed calls. I couldn't believe Dalvin hadn't called me. I couldn't help but wonder if he was still pissed at me for what I considered our "minor confrontation" when he dropped me off this afternoon. I was anxious to speak to him, but I was also famished. I decided to sneak downstairs and get something to eat, and then call Dalvin once I had calmed down the hunger pains coming from my stomach.

After unlocking my bedroom door and opening it, I just knew a whole army of bodyguards would be waiting to take me to my dad. I was relieved and surprised when the hallway was completely empty. I tiptoed down the wraparound stairs, keeping my eyes roaming and my ears open, and still no one was in sight.

When I was about to reach the kitchen, I heard low voices that sounded like my dad and mother's coming from my dad's office. Curious to know what they were talking about, I walked towards his office. The door was slightly ajar, and as I got closer, their voices became clearer.

"Ronny, I know you feel like keeping Mercedes away from Dalvin is the right thing to do, but I'm worried it might backfire."

"I know my baby girl. She'll come around. She's a little upset right now, but trust me, Mercedes don't ever let me down," my dad said confidently.

"But this time is different. Your little girl has never been in love."

"Latoya, I know Mercedes better than anybody. She don't love that boy. How could she? He ain't good enough for her. My daughter has gone to the best schools and is top of the line quality. She would never get caught up in some street thug."

"Ronny, you don't see the similarities between you and Dalvin? Just like I fell for you, Mercedes has fallen for him."

"Toy, Mercedes isn't you. Yeah, she has your beauty, but that's where it stops,"

I peeped my head further in the door because I wanted to catch a glimpse of my parents' faces.

"You don't have the education or the class that Mercedes has. It's not your fault, because you grew up in the projects your whole life. Mercedes was raised better than that. She's going to marry a doctor or a lawyer, someone who has the same grooming as her."

My mother put her head down, obviously crushed by what my dad said. Now I understood why she never felt she would be good enough. "Whether or not Mercedes has more class than me don't matter. Love don't care about class, it goes by what the heart feels. I know that look Mercedes has in her eyes, because I had it when I told my mother I was pregnant and going to live with you. Just like you think Mercedes is too good for Dalvin, yeah, I was from the projects, but my mother wanted better for me than to be pregnant at fifteen by a drug dealer."

My dad just stood there looking at my moms. I couldn't begin to figure out what was going on in his head. In my mind, I was still digesting that my mom called daddy a drug dealer. I had never heard her call him that before.

"Enough of this. Mercedes won't be seeing Dalvin, and that's that," he said, sitting down at his desk and letting my mother know the conversation was over.

"You gon' lose Mercedes."

"Excuse me?" he asked with astonishment in his voice.

I swallowed hard because I was stunned that my mother would even have the guts to go there with my dad.

"I mean, you should try to work things out with her before it's too late."

Right when I thought my mom's had some backbone, she once again backed off from my dad, not saying what she really thought. Because it was true. If my dad insisted on me ending my relationship with Dalvin, he would lose me, and my mother knew it. But instead of keeping it real and sticking to that, she couldn't take the heat and tried to smooth it over with my dad. I had heard enough, and bounced before I was noticed. Plus, I had to sneak some snacks out of the kitchen.

When I opened the refrigerator, my eyes immediately went to the chicken Parmesan our cook had made. It was one of my favorites, but I would be taking a serious chance of getting caught if I heated it up, so I just grabbed a soda. Then I raided the cabinet and took the Doritos, cupcakes and granola bars. By the time I got back to my bedroom, I had already demolished half of the junk. As I unwrapped my second cupcake, I heard a slight knock at the door. I gathered my goodies and put them under my bed. "Who is it?"

"It's me."

"Ma, I'm really not in the mood for company."

"I thought you might be hungry, so I brought you up some dinner. It's one of your favorites, chicken Parmesan."

My eyes got big, because eating all this junk food made me want something hot in my stomach. I got up, unlocked the door, and then sat back down on my bed. "It's open," I said nonchalantly, not wanting to appear too happy to get the meal.

My mother came in with the tray in her hands. She

had even put a little flower in a vase to give it that special touch.

"You can just put it over there on my desk." I kept my head down, not making eye contact with her.

"Mercedes, stop frontin' like you're not dying to eat this food and get your butt over here."

I couldn't help but crack a smile. I practically skipped over to the food. The aroma was filling the air, and I knew how good it was gonna taste on my tongue.

"It wouldn't hurt for you to say thank you."

"Thanks, Ma."

"You're welcome. I hope this means that tomorrow you'll be coming out your room."

"I haven't decided yet. But, Ma, can we talk about this after I finish eating?"

I figured my mother would leave and come back later, but instead, she scooted the two throw pillows to the side and sat on my cream chaise, and sat there until I finished my meal. After continuing to slurp on my juice even after there was nothing left, she finally had enough. "Mercedes, it's all gone. Now stop avoiding me and tell me how we can resolve all this craziness."

"That's simple. You and Daddy can let me still see Dalvin."

"You know your Dad isn't goin' to agree to that."

"And why not?"

"Because he doesn't believe Dalvin is good for you. And after you snuck out this house last night, he's probably right."

"No, he's not. If Daddy hadn't thrown Dalvin out like he was some dangerous criminal that would've never happened. Ma, I would think you'd understand where I'm comin' from. I just want to be with the guy that I love."

"I do understand, Mercedes, more than you know. But I also know how stubborn your Dad is, and he's not goin' to change his mind. So, in order for this family to have peace, I'm begging you to stop seeing Dalvin."

I studied my mom's face before I responded. Her voice sounded sincere, but her eyes told a different story. "I'm sorry, but I won't be able to do that. Now, could you please leave? I'm tired and I want to go to bed."

My mother got up and picked up my dinner tray. She walked towards my door, and then paused and looked back at me. "You might want to be with Dalvin now, but being in love with a street thug will bring more pain and heartache than joy. Trust me, I know." With that, my mother left.

Right after she closed the door, I heard my cell phone ringing. It was Dalvin. It's about time! I said to myself.

"Baby, where you been?"

"Just dealing wit' some things. I'm on my way to pick you up. I need to see my baby."

"Dalvin, it's almost midnight, I can't leave the house now."

"Oh, you mean you can't leave to come see me?"

"It wouldn't matter if you were a choir boy, my parents wouldn't let me leave the house this time of night."

"Whateva, man!"

"Don't be like that. You know I want to see you. I've been callin' you all day, but your phone kept goin' to voice mail. I miss you, but I just can't."

"Why can't you sneak out like last night? I'll make sure you get home early before anybody wakes up."

"That's what I wanted to talk to you about. I had a blow up with my mom's when I came home. I told her the truth, that I spent the night with you." There was dead silence on the phone. "Hello?" I finally said.

"I'm here. You told her that?"

"Yeah, I did, and I've been locked up in my room ever since. I wanted her to know that I love you, and that they can't keep us apart. But I know they're goin' to be extra tight with security since I snuck out."

"I hear you. Mercedes, I'm just not used to this. How can I not see my girl when I want to? But then, you're young, and I'm used to dealing with females that can come and go as they please. This situation is different."

Dalvin was making me feel worse. Now he was coming at me like I was some little girl. I know he wasn't trying to hurt my feelings, but he was. "So why you gotta make my age an issue? When you was making love to me last night you wasn't screaming about how young I was."

"Because your age is an issue. If you was eighteen, then you could do what you wanted to do, and all this sneaking around wouldn't be necessary."

"But, Dalvin, you're not even eighteen."

"No need to be. My parents ain't got no leash on me like I'm some kid."

"Baby, please, can you stop? I don't wanna argue with you. Last night I gave you the most precious thing I have, and now you making me feel like I made a mistake."

"Mercedes, no. I wanna see you so bad. I miss you. Not being able to hold you right now is pissing me off. Call me selfish. I wish we could dash off right now and get married so I could run your life and tell you what to do." As I started laughing, Dalvin cut me off. "Laugh if you want to, but I'm serious."

"I know. I wish I could marry you too. It was just how you said it. I've never met anybody so open as to say what they want."

"How else am I supposed to get it, if I don't let it be known that I want it? And I want you to be my wife, so it shall be."

"You really wanna marry me?" I knew that we were in love and that I wanted to marry him since the moment I saw him, but never did I think he would want me to be his wife.

"Mercedes, you're unlike any girl I ever met. If I don't get you now, then pretty soon your mind will become corrupted by all the garbage out here in these streets. Why would I take the chance of lettin' that happen, when I know you're perfect for me? My parents have been married forever, just like yours. I have to make you mine while you're still young so I can mold you."

I knew Dalvin sounded like a male chauvinist, but I didn't care. I actually thought it was cute. "Baby, I love you so much. I hope one day we can get married."

"I got this. Now get some sleep, I'll call you tomorrow."

"Okay, I love you."

"I love you too."

I lay in my bed, staring up at the ceiling. I imagined Dalvin and I having the flyest wedding, with me dressed to the nines in some couture type wedding gown, with a crazy rock sitting heavy on my finger. Then, being escorted in on some horse and carriage, over the top scenario. Rose petals at my feet leading to my prince, and the best part, my dad walking me down the aisle. It all seemed farfetched now, but nothing was impossible, especially when that was what your heart desired. I fell asleep dreaming of just that, and was determined to make my dream a reality.

"Girl, wake up!" I heard Keisha screaming while playfully mashing a pillow over my head.

"I hear you, now chill!" I really didn't want to wake up, especially since I was in the middle of visualizing the last kiss Dalvin and I shared.

"Nah, I won't stop."

I finally opened my eyes, with the vision of Keisha standing before me with her hands resting on her ample hips. "Yeah, you need to wake up. Locking your door all day yesterday, not lettin' nobody in. I'm your partner in crime. How you gonna keep me out?"

"Keisha, it's entirely too early for this."

"It's not early, it's one o'clock. You lucky I let you sleep this long, but Auntie Toy told me y'all had a little discussion last night, so I figured you might be stressed."

"How kind of you, but all this noise comin' from your mouth is what's really stressing me." I glanced over at the clock. "Is my dad here?"

"No, he left about an hour ago."

"Good. I'm not ready to talk to him."

"Well, you betta start being ready, 'cause he has a few words for you."

"What do you mean?"

"You know Auntie Toy told him you snuck out the other night to be wit' D. He was furious. But of course, you're his little princess, so he blamed it all on D."

"Go get dressed. We goin' out."

"Out where?"

"The mall, now let's go!"

That was the one place that would get Keisha up and ready in a heartbeat. Within an hour, we were downstairs, ready to bolt, but I had to get past my mother first.

"Where do you think you going?"

"To the mall."

"I'll take you."

"I don't need you takin' me to the mall."

"Your dad doesn't want you leaving the house unsupervised."

"Oh, is it because you told him that I snuck out to see Dalvin?"

My mom's gave Keisha a scathing look, and turned back at me. "You left me no choice, Mercedes."

"You always have a choice, and you always choose Daddy. But I am goin' to the mall. So unless you want to hold me down like a prisoner, I'm leavin'."

"Fine! The two of you go to the mall, but come straight home afterwards."

"We will."

As soon as I got in the car and started driving off, I called Dalvin.

"What you doin'?" Keisha inquired, since I was swerving while trying to pick up my cell that I dropped on the side of my seat.

"About to get my man on the phone."

"I shoulda known you was callin' D."

"Chill, Keisha! I'm still takin' you to the mall," I smacked while dialing Dalvin's number. "Hi, baby,"

"What's goin' on, pretty girl?"

"You. I'm with Keisha and we're goin' to the mall. Can you meet me there?"

"No doubt! I'm right in that area, so hit me when you get here."

"Girl, you playin' wit' fire. Auntie Toy is gonna kill you."

"For what? We are goin' to the mall. How was I supposed to know that Dalvin was gonna be there too?

It's a free country."

"Boy, oh boy, you really strung out on this guy. I never thought you'd love another man more than your daddy."

"What? What type of mess is that to say?"

"I'm saying, I always thought you'd be a daddy's little girl, but since you've fallen for D, it's like all bets are off."

There was silence for the remainder of the car ride as I thought about what Keisha said. It was true. Pleasing my dad was no longer a priority for me. I was more concerned about how Dalvin felt. Although I didn't want to hurt my dad, I just wanted to be with Dalvin more. I mean, Dalvin was the man that I gave my virginity to. That meant we shared a bond that I hoped would last forever.

When I pulled into the parking garage, I was able to get a prime spot right in the front.

"Girl, we lucked out. I'm so happy we don't have to walk all far."

"I knew you would be happy. Hold on one sec, let me call Dalvin and let him know where we are."

"You can't walk and dial a number at the same time?" Keisha was steady walking ahead of me, twisting her behind like she had an attitude.

"You need some help?" I heard a male voice ask as I struggled to multi-task with my cell phone and car keys.

"I'm good, but thanks," I said as I dropped my keys. "I'm a little clumsy."

"Don't worry about it," he said, picking up my keys and handing them to me. "You're very pretty. Do you think I can take you out sometime?"

"Nah, I have a boyfriend."

"I should've known. But how about takin' my number, just in case your man stops appreciating what he has?" Before I could tell the guy no thanks, Dalvin stormed up like he was vexed.

"Yo, step away from my girl!"

"Dalvin, chill. He was just handing me my car keys."

"No disrespect, man, I thought she could use some help."

"A'ight, preppy, you can keep it movin' now." Dalvin eyed the guy down while he walked away.

"What was that all about? He was just giving me my keys."

"So he wasn't tryna get wit' you?"

"No."

"Oh, so you like to lie to me like you do your parents?"

"Where is all this comin' from?"

"I stood right over there and heard that cat ask you for your number, even after you told him you had a man."

"Dalvin, that didn't mean nothin'."

"So, why didn't you just say that? Why you gotta lie to me about it?"

"I didn't want you gettin' all worked up over nothin'."

"Mercedes, I can't stand a liar. Don't lie to me. I don't care how minuscule you think it is. A liar lacks character."

Dalvin's words made me feel ashamed. I had been lying to my parents since I started dating him. I lied to my mother not even an hour ago so I could creep off and be with him. It's like once the lies start, they never stop. But what could I do? My back was against the wall.

"Baby, I understand. I'm sorry, I should've been honest. I really didn't think it was a big deal, but still, there was no reason to lie to you about it."

"That's cool, just don't lie to me again. Now, give

me a kiss."

I lifted my head up and relished in the softness of his lips.

"Are we goin' in the mall or what?" Keisha bellowed, getting increasingly tired of waiting.

"Can you hold up a minute? I'm waiting for Demetrius."

"I didn't know Demetrius was with you."

"Now you want to change up your tone and sound all sweet 'cause you know my man is comin'."

"Can you blame me? I can't take but so much of all this lovey-dovey mess."

"But it's cool for all that when you cozy up with Demetrius?" I said, checking Keisha's simple-acting self.

Once Demetrius appeared, of course Keisha became chipper, and all the complaining went out the window.

After a couple of hours of holding hands and walking around the mall, I was ready to leave and do something else.

Just when I was going to share my thoughts with Dalvin, my cell phone started ringing. I looked to see who was calling, and opted not to answer.

"Who was that?" he asked.

"My mother."

"Why didn't you pick up?"

"Because I knew she would be asking me a million questions, and I'm not in the mood to answer them."

"A million questions like what?"

"Stuff. I told her I was goin' to the mall, but I didn't tell her I was meeting you."

"So, you still lyin' about us?"

Before Dalvin started riffing, I jumped to the next subject. "Let's get outta here. I've been dreaming of us being intimate again since you dropped me off at home the other day."

"Mercedes, you think I'm so hard up that I'm goin' to ignore the fact you ducking your mother because you still lyin' about us?"

I put my hand on my forehead as I let out a deep sigh.

"That's why I don't even like dealing wit' young girls, 'cause your so childish."

"I forgot you like mature girls like Fatima. I can't compete with that, now can I?" I vented derisively.

"Fatima was never my girl. I kicked it wit' her a couple of times, and she got the relationship twisted. But this is about you."

"I don't know what to say, Dalvin. My parents have made it clear that they don't want me seeing you. What am I supposed to do?"

"Tell them the truth. That we love each other and they can't keep us apart."

"You make it sound so easy."

"It is."

"I still haven't met your parents yet. Do you think they'll be so understanding when they find out who my father is?"

"There's only one way to find out. Let's go." Dalvin grabbed me by my arm and then nodded for Demetrius and Keisha to come on. He wasn't saying two words, just walking like he was on a mission. "Give me your car keys."

"Where we goin'?"

"Just give me your keys."

I reluctantly handed them over, feeling a little nervous by how intense Dalvin was acting. He walked over to Demetrius, said a few words, and then got in the car. He drove off, still not saying a word. For most of the drive, I had my head down, pondering about how just the other night Dalvin seemed so in love with me, and now I seemed to be getting on his last nerves.

In the midst of my thinking, I glanced up and realized that we were in Highland Park, entering an exclusive lakefront property on acres of land. I looked behind me and saw Demetrius pulling up behind us in the Range.

"Dalvin, where are you takin' me?"

"To meet my parents."

I couldn't help but be in awe at the opulent estate. It was equal, if not a tad better, than the spread I lived on.

"I knew Dalvin was official, but this is beyond top notch," Keisha stated as she shook her head back and forth.

"Mercedes, Keisha, let's go."

We followed behind Dalvin, studying every detail of his family's lavish home. The statement my daddy used to say all the time to me when I was growing up kept ringing in my head: "Mo' money, mo' problems." With this type of digs, the problems had to be endless.

When we entered the grand foyer with inlaid marble floors leading to the double spiral staircase to upper and lower levels, I was amazed by just how lucrative the business my dad and Dalvin's father were in.

The maid entered the foyer greeting us. "Mr. Dalvin, would you and your guests care for anything?"

"Not right now, Selena. Do you know where my mother is?"

"Yes, outside in the gazebo."

"Thank you."

As we made our way outside, I continued to be impressed with how exquisitely decorated the home was. From the distance, I could see who I assumed was Dalvin's mother sitting alone, admiring the lakefront view. The landscaping was impeccable, and I began getting nervous as we got closer.

The woman's eyes lit up when she saw Dalvin. "Hi, baby! I wasn't expecting you anytime soon," the regal woman said, giving Dalvin a hug.

"I know, Mother, but I wanted you to meet someone." His mother looked over in my direction, staring at both Keisha, and me I assume trying to figure out which one was there for her son. "Mother, this is Mercedes. Mercedes, this is my mother."

"It's a pleasure to meet you," I said, feeling even more nervous once I met her up close.

She had a presence of royalty. She appeared to be about ten years older than my mother, but just as beautiful. She was so refined, and that doesn't come from designer clothes or expensive jewelry, that's from your pedigree. To my surprise, she walked over to me and gave me a hug. "Aren't you a beautiful, young lady. If I didn't know better, I would think you were a daughter of mine," she said with an endearing chuckle.

"That's funny, 'cause I be tellin' them all the time they look like brother and sister," Keisha chimed in.

At first I wasn't sure how such a majestic woman would take to Keisha's around the way girl demeanor, but if it did bother her, she didn't let us know it. "Now, what is your name? I love a girl who isn't afraid to speak up."

"Keisha. I'm Mercedes' cousin. I'm also dating Demetrius," she added.

"How nice. Would you ladies like something to drink?"

"I'm good," I said.

"You have any sweet tea? I'm a little thirsty,"

Keisha asked.

"Of course, dear. I'll call up to Selena."

"Mrs. Dewitt, that's okay, I'll take Keisha inside to get the tea."

"Are you sure, Demetrius?"

"Yes, ma'am."

I saw the look Dalvin gave Demetrius, and knew it was his idea for Demetrius to make the suggestion. I figured he wanted us to have some alone time with his mother.

"Mother, the reason I brought Mercedes over here is because..."

Dalvin's mother cut him off. "Obviously because she's extremely special to you," she said, looking at me. "Mercedes, you're the first girl my son has ever brought over to meet me, and I know he has dallied with quite a few," she chuckled. "So, for him to bring you to our home, he must have deep feelings for you."

"I appreciate that, because I have very strong feelings for your son."

"Actually, Mother, we're in love."

Right after Dalvin made that statement, we all turned our heads to the sound of someone walking up. Standing before me was a man who was the replica of Dalvin, only older.

"Dad, I'm so glad you're here." Dalvin got the biggest grin on his face when he saw his father. They gave each other an interlocking arm hug

"You must be Mercedes. My son has spoken very highly of you."

"Yes, I am. He speaks very highly of you too."

"You're far more beautiful than my son described, wouldn't you agree, Miriam?"

Dalvin's mother smiled and nodded her head, yes.

"Dad, Mercedes and I are in a bit of a dilemma."

"What seems to be the problem, son?"

"I didn't have a chance to tell you this, but her father is Ronald Clinton."

"The Ronald Clinton?"

"Yes."

My stomach was doing somersaults. I wasn't expecting Dalvin to be so upfront with everything, and I was afraid that Mr. Dewitt was going to toss me out his house the same way my father did Dalvin.

"So, you're Ronny's little girl. You're not so little anymore. I remember years ago, I met you one time. Your father had a huge birthday party when you turned five. Elephants, horses and monkeys, you name it. He brought the circus to your backyard."

"You were there? Did you bring Dalvin?"

"No, I was on my way out of town and had something important to discuss with your father before I left. I could barely get a good five minutes out of him, because he didn't want to be apart from you. He truly adored you. You were such a pretty little girl, and now you've grown into a beautiful young lady."

"Thank you for saying that."

"No, thank you. I couldn't imagine a girl more ideal for my son."

This wasn't the response I was expecting from Dalvin's parents. This was like night and day.

"I'm happy you feel that way, Dad."

"I assume Ronny doesn't feel the same way?"

"He's forbidden me to see Dalvin anymore. But I love your son so much. If you don't mind me asking, why does he have such a problem with you?"

"It's a long story, Mercedes, but you know. The mo' money you make, the mo' problems you have. And as you can see, both I and your father have made plenty of money. But your father shouldn't let our differences interfere with you and Dalvin's happiness."

"I told him the same thing, but he doesn't want to hear it."

"Dad, Mercedes' parents don't know that she's with me today. She lied to them, and I explained to her that lying is a character flaw that I'm not comfortable with. I told her she needs to be honest with her parents, the way I'm honest with you."

"I've tried to be honest with my parents, but they don't want to hear it."

"I can't tell you what to do, but I believe you should be honest with them and stand your ground. There's no sense in lying, because the truth always comes to the light."

"Mr. Dewitt, what if they still try to keep me from Dalvin? Then what?"

"Only you have the answer to that."

"My dear, love is the only gift in life that truly stands the test of time. Only you know how much you love Dalvin, and what you're willing to sacrifice for that love."

Mrs. Dewitt's words hit a core with me. How much would I sacrifice for love?

Chapter 7

Stand Off

When Keisha and I arrived home, I was immediately greeted by my parents. From the solemn look on both of their faces, I knew they weren't pleased with me. I didn't want to go to war with them, but I also had no intention of being bullied either.

"Where have you been?" were the first words out of my dad's mouth.

"It's nice to see you too, Daddy," I said coyly.

My dad stared at me intently while I walked towards the kitchen as if nothing was wrong. I could hear their footsteps following me to my destination.

"Where have you been?" my dad asked once again, this time with extra bass in his voice.

If he was trying to get my full attention, he had it. With my hand on the refrigerator handle, I stopped and made eye contact with him, and then my mother. Keisha was lingering in the back, trying to stay out the line of fire. I took a deep breath before answering.

"I went to the mall with Keisha."

I noticed my mother rolling her eyes as she crossed her arms. That was a clear indication that she knew there was a part two that I was leaving out. I was debating in my head just how much they knew or whether I was just being paranoid.

The next thing I peeped was Keisha completely missing from the scene. She knew that the next question from my dad was going to be directed at her. As expected, he turned around in search of my cousin, who was now ghost. "Where's Keisha? Maybe she can tell me where you all have been."

"Daddy, I just told you," I responded innocently.

"So, you haven't been with Dalvin?" he asked point blank, deciding to stop with the guessing games.

I started biting down on my bottom lip, knowing that it was about to be on. One thing I knew about my dad, he had a lawyer's approach when it came to questions; never ask one unless you already know the answer. With that in mind, I began mentally preparing myself for the showdown.

"Yes, I was with Dalvin today."

My mother's eyes got big as I admitted the truth. I guess she thought that I would lie to the bitter end, but I decided against continuing the deceit after meeting with Dalvin's parents. I think my dad was also shocked that he didn't have to drag the truth out of me, because he stood there speechless, as if he didn't hear what I said.

"I forbade you to see him again. How could you go against my wishes?"

"What, you think I can turn off my feelings for Dalvin just like that? You don't understand. I love him."

"More than you love your family?"

"This isn't about choosing between my family and Dalvin. His parents accept me, why can't you accept him?" I don't know if it was because of all the heat in the kitchen, but I would've sworn I saw smoke coming from dad's head.

"When did you meet his parents?" My mother asked the question that my dad couldn't seem to.

"Today. Dalvin wanted to show me that his parents would embrace me and not have a problem with our relationship, unlike the two of you."

"How dare you step foot in the home of my enemy!" my daddy finally said with vengeance in his voice.

"Daddy, I don't understand you. Because Mr. Dewitt is your enemy, I have to stop lovin' Dalvin? You're asking me to do the impossible."

"I'm not asking you, I'm telling you to be loyal to your family."

"This has nothin' to do with being loyal. This is about following my heart. I'm in love and want to spend the rest of my life with Dalvin."

"That can never happen. All your life I told you, mo' money, mo' problems. Well, being with Dalvin is a major problem. His father and I have our hands in the same pie, vying for the same money. This is about business, and I will not have a daughter of mine involved with the son of the man that is my enemy in business."

"Oh, so this is about you, your money and your business. You, you, you! What about me and how I feel? But I guess that's irrelevant to you," I belted.

"Mercedes, calm down. You don't speak to your father like that."

Everything inside of me wanted to walk over and smack my mother. I was so sick of her constantly defending my dad as if he was unable to defend himself, which was a joke within itself.

Sensing that his "take no prisoners" approach wasn't working, my dad tried another angle. "Mercedes, just excuse your mother. She doesn't understand that you don't mean to yell at me."

Behind my dad's back, my mother was giving him the look of disgust after what he said. But she would never have the balls to do it in his face.

"I know that when you think you're in love, your emotions can get the best of you. So you're getting yourself all worked up, and I forgive you."

Now I didn't know who I couldn't stand more, my arrogant dad or passive mom. Both of them made me want to vomit. "I appreciate your forgiveness, Daddy, but it doesn't change anything unless you're now giving me your blessings with my relationship with Dalvin."

"I can't do that."

"You mean you won't." My dad began pacing back and forth, as if in deep thought.

"I honestly thought I could spare you from this, but you're not leaving me a choice."

I couldn't help but wonder what angle my dad was going to play next.

"Mercedes, all your life I described my profession as an entrepreneur, which I am, but many other people would label me a criminal. I have a lot of legitimate businesses, but they're mostly a cover-up for the millions I make illegally."

As I listened to my dad finally reveal the truth about his profession, I was tempted to tell him that Dalvin had already schooled me on his criminal world. But I figured I shouldn't rain on his attempt to come clean.

"Okay, Daddy, I understand why you wouldn't want me to know about your criminal activities. But it doesn't make me love you any less."

"I appreciate that, baby girl," he said smoothly, feeling that he was making progress. "So, then you can comprehend why it concerns me who you're involved with. Being with someone like Dalvin is very dangerous, because his family is also part of the same criminal world."

"But Mother married you."

"That's different."

"How?"

"I was the only future your mother had, but the world is your oyster. I've provided you with the ammunition to have anything in this world that you want."

"Well, I want Dalvin," I stated firmly, refusing to cave in to my father's demands.

"He's a crook! What don't you understand about that?"

"I understand that perfectly, because you're a crook too. But just like I still love and respect you in spite of how you make your living, I have that same unconditional love for Dalvin."

"How can you even make a comparison between me and that lowdown thug? He's beneath you."

"Ma, you've been awfully quiet. Do you agree with that?" I decided to bring her into the fold since she married the exact type of man my father was making Dalvin out to be. She glanced over at my dad before answering.

"Your father knows best."

"You hear that, Daddy? Mother has always stood right by your side, defending you whether you're right or wrong. But I'm not sleeping with you, I'm sleeping with Dalvin. So I refuse to bow down to you like Mother does, even if it means turning her back on her own daughter."

Without warning, my father leaped at me and began shaking me uncontrollably. My mother seemed too stunned to move, or maybe she thought I was getting what I deserved. My body started getting weak and I wanted to break free from his clutches, but his strength was overpowering me. As I became dizzy, I could no longer understand what my dad was saying. His words started fading.

"Ronny, stop! You're hurting her!" I barely heard my mother scream.

My father ignored her until he realized my body was going limp. "Dear God, what have I done?" he said, lifting me up in his arms and then laying me down on top of the kitchen table. "Latoya, get a glass of water." I could hear my mother frantically rumbling to get a glass and pouring the water.

"Here," she said breathlessly.

"Drink this, Mercedes," my dad insisted as he tried to force the water down my throat. His fear that I had lost consciousness was getting the better of him.

"What's goin' on in here?" I heard Keisha ask. "Omigoodness! What happened to Mercedes?"

"Keisha, please, this ain't the time for questions," my mother spewed.

I began coughing as the water got caught in my throat. The energy it took to cough got my adrenaline pumping at full speed again. My head felt as if a train wreck happened inside my brain. With my mind becoming more focused, I quickly remembered who put me in this predicament.

"Get away from me!" I demanded, sliding my body off the table.

"Mercedes, I'm so sorry. You know I would never intentionally hurt you. I snapped when you said you had sex with that boy." He muttered the last few words as if it was killing him to say them.

My mother ran towards me, trying to put her arms

around me, but I brushed her off. Before they could stop me, I grabbed my purse and ran out the house. As I drove off, I kept replaying the exchange of words that led up to my dad shaking me deliriously.

My dad had never put his hands on me. Come to think of it, neither had my mother, except for her recent slap. I was always a reasonable child and never second-guessed my dad. Maybe that was why defying him by not ending my relationship with Dalvin was sending him over the edge.

After driving around for over an hour, I finally went to the place I felt I would be wanted.

"I'm so glad you came," Mrs. Dewitt said, opening the door for me.

After Dalvin's cell phone went straight to voice mail, I called his house. His mother answered the phone and told me Dalvin wasn't home, but to my surprise, she invited me to come over anyway.

"Thank you for having me."

"A young lady that my son is so fond of is always welcome in our home." It was obvious that Dalvins' parents truly cared about his happiness. I wished my parents could be so understanding. "Selena just finished preparing dinner. Would you like something to eat?"

"Yes, I'm starving." Right before I was about to feed my face at home, the altercation broke out with my dad, dissolving those plans. I hoped a good meal would calm my nerves.

"Well, let's eat."

I didn't say two words to Mrs. Dewitt over dinner. I was too busy devouring the lobster tails, shrimp and scallops. Whatever sauce Selena used was finger licking good, literally. I knew Mrs. Dewitt must've thought I looked like a stray dog that hadn't had a meal in days, but the food was banging, and I was starving. The combination of those two things made it impossible for me to eat with any sort of sophistication.

"Wow, Mrs. Dewitt! That was delicious!" I managed to say after swallowing the last of my juice.

"You weren't lying when you said you were starving. I'm happy you enjoyed the meal," she commented with a warm smile. "Now that your stomach is full, do you feel like telling me what had you so upset earlier?"

"It's a long story."

"I'm not going anywhere."

I really didn't want to discuss my family drama with Mrs. Dewitt. She was such a classy lady and I felt embarrassed by what had taken place at home. But at the same time, she'd been so kind, and I felt she deserved an explanation. "This is a little hard for me to talk about."

"I'm sure it is. But if you're worried about me judging you, don't. I've been on this earth for a good amount of time, and trust me, mama has lived. I've had more than my share of dramatic episodes."

It was amazing how she seemed to read my mind, or maybe the shame was written on my face. Whatever it was, she made me feel at ease to open up to her.

"I had a huge blow up with my parents. When I got home, they confronted me about Dalvin. I was tired of lying, so I admitted that I had been with him even after my dad had warned me not to. From there, it went from bad to worse. My dad almost shook me to death." I paused for a minute, waiting for Mrs. Dewitt's mouth to drop, and then tell me how despicable my father was for behaving that way, which in turn, would make me want to defend him because, he was my dad and I still loved him.

"I'm sure your father didn't mean to hurt you. Because your parents love you so much, sometimes they act without thinking of the consequences of their actions. I know we're supposed to be the adults, but we're human and make mistakes just like our kids do."

I was dumbfounded at how she rationalized what had taken place with my dad.

"You look so stunned. What did you expect me to say?"

"I thought you would tell me what a horrible person my dad is."

"I would never do that. That's your father. A daughter and a father's relationship runs deep."

"Yeah, my dad and I have always been close until he found out about Dalvin. He's trying to make me choose between them, and it isn't fair."

"Nothing is fair in love, my dear. My father, may he rest in peace, was a well-respected judge in Chicago. The day I told him I was in love with Dalvin, he vowed to use all his political power to destroy him if I didn't end the relationship. When I refused to leave him, he cut me off financially and I was ostracized from my family. I was in college at the time, and from the stress of it, all I wanted to do was drop out, but Dalvin wouldn't let me. He paid my tuition, insisting that my education was too important. Eventually, we married, but it didn't deter my father from stopping his mission of bringing my husband down. My father couldn't fathom why a daughter who'd come from so much could fall in love with a known criminal."

"So, what ended up happenin'?"

"He had Dalvin arrested a few times on charges that could never stick. The one case against him that did make it to court, Dalvin beat at trial."

"What was your mother saying when all of this was going on?"

"Unfortunately, nothing. She died when I was fourteen and my father never remarried. I think that was another reason why he fought so hard to keep me close. But his determination to break me and Dalvin up only made us drift apart."

"So you all never reunited?"

"Yes, but not until after I had Dalvin. He was so proud to have a grandson, he swallowed all of his pride and anger so that he could be a part of his life."

"How did your husband take that?"

"Surprisingly, he was so forgiving. He would always say that he understood how my father felt, because if he had a daughter like me, he would do whatever necessary to protect her too."

"Wow, that's incredible!"

"Yes it is. To this day, it still breaks my heart that I lost so much time with my father. He passed away from heart complications when Dalvin was only three years old. If only he hadn't shut me out for so long. But I cherished everyday of those three years that I had with him."

"Do you ever regret choosing your husband over your father?"

"I didn't consider it a choice. My heart belonged to Dalvin. I knew my future was with him. To not be with him would've meant that I chose not to live."

Mrs. Dewitt's words were so potent. In my heart I felt that same love for her son.

"I so desperately want my dad to accept Dalvin, because I love them both so much. Is there any advice you can give me?"

"Follow your heart. All the answers are inside of

you. But, no matter what choice you make, never give up on trying to maintain a loving relationship with your father. He's the only one you have."

"Mercedes, what are you doin' here?" Dalvin asked with a confused grin on his face.

"I'll leave you two alone. You have a lot to talk about."

"Thank you for listening to me, Mrs. Dewitt."

"No, thank you." She gave me a hug and walked out of the kitchen.

"Your mother is so amazing."

"Yeah, she a'ight," Dalvin said, jokingly. "So, what's goin' on? I was mad confused when I saw your car parked out front."

"I tried to call you earlier to let you know what was goin' on, but your phone kept goin' straight to voicemail. It does that a lot. Is that how our relationship is goin' to always be, not being able to get you on the phone for whatever reason?"

"If you think I be wit' other girls, you're mistaken. That's not the case at all."

"What am I supposed to think?"

"The truth. When I'm handling business, most of the time I'm unavailable. But if an emergency comes up and you have to get at me, I'll always make that possible for you. You need to know that this is my life."

"This doesn't have to be your life. Your father has so much money that he can set you up with whatever business you want."

"Let me rephrase that then. This is the life that I want. My father has hustled all his life so that I wouldn't have to, but I can't help it. I'm his son and it's in my blood. You have to accept that if you wanna be wit' me.

That ain't gon' neva change."

"So, you're sayin' you would choose your business over me?"

"No, my business is part of who I am. It was who I was before I met you, and it will still be me if you left me ten years from now. So, to ask me to stop would be asking me to give up a part of who I am. I would never ask that of you."

"Baby, I don't want you to change. I want you to be you, that's who I fell in love with."

"Are you sure? Because this life isn't pretty. The money's good, but the level of intensity is high. Your father has always protected you from this street life. If you're with me, of course I'll keep by business separate from you as much as possible. But sometimes I'ma need a confidante, and I want my wife to be that person."

"You'll always be able to confide in me, no matter what. My loyalty will be with you."

"Then come give your future husband a hug."

It felt so right being in Dalvin's arms. Feeling his love made me know I made the right decision by being honest with my parents.

"I love you so much, baby."

"I love you too. Now, tell me what happened with your parents. I know that's the only thing that can have you over here pouring your heart out to Mom."

With that, I heated up a plate of food for Dalvin, and as he ate his dinner, I recounted the standoff between my father and me.

Chapter 8

Final Goodbye

When I woke up the next morning, for a moment I forgot where I was. It felt weird opening my eyes and being in a strange bedroom. Waking up with Dalvin next to me would've made it a lot easier, but that was out the question.

Although he swore his parents would be cool with us sleeping in the same room, I told him, "No way." I felt it would be totally disrespectful, and I didn't want his parents thinking I was some hot in the pants teenager. Especially since I held his mother in such high esteem.

While lying in bed looking at the posh furniture and exquisite paintings on the wall, I heard a knock at the door. I sat up and tried to fluff out my hair and do face stretches so I wouldn't have that I just woke up look.

"Come in."

"Good morning, Mercedes."

"Good morning, Mrs. Dewitt." I did a quick glance at the clock and saw it was just nine o'clock. "I'm surprised you're up so early." I was actually more surprised that I was up. During the summer I rarely got out of bed before eleven. But I did have a lot on my mind, and literally tossed and turned all night.

"Dear, I'm an early bird. I've been that way ever

since I can remember."

Although I believed Mrs. Dewitt was telling the truth, I couldn't help but wonder if she was also checking to see if her son had somehow found his way into my bed in the middle of the night. Luckily he hadn't.

"Well, I love to sleep late."

"So does Dalvin. I didn't expect you to be up, but I'm glad that you are. If you don't mind, I would love if you joined me for breakfast."

"I'd like that. Just give me a minute to pull it together."

"Take your time. I'll see you downstairs."

I stepped out of bed and headed to the bathroom. When I entered, the first thing I noticed were all the new toiletries. I figured they kept every bathroom stocked for their guests. It was too bad that I hadn't come prepared with a change of clothes. The last thing I wanted to do was put on what I wore yesterday. After washing my face, brushing my teeth and putting on my clothes, I headed downstairs.

Mrs. Dewitt was seated at the dining table, sipping on tea and reading the newspaper. I thought about my mother, and with all the fashion magazines I watched her flip through, I'd never seen her read the newspaper.

"Mercedes, have a seat," Mrs. Dewitt said as she looked up from her reading.

When I sat down, I couldn't help but to keep thinking about my own mother. I knew she was probably worried about me and angry at the same time. I felt that maybe I should call her, but I still didn't want to hear her voice.

"Mercedes, I know that you're probably still upset with your parents, but you know they have to be concerned about you."

"I know," I said before picking up my glass of

freshly squeezed orange juice.

"You should really give them a call."

"I'm sure you're ready for me to go home, and I will." I figured Mrs. Dewitt didn't want me up under her son too much longer, and was trying to convince me to call my parents so I could get out her house. I wanted to reassure her that I planned on doing just that. I just needed a little more time.

"My dear, you can stay as long as you like. I mean that." Her eyes did have the look of sincerity. "You must understand, I'm a parent too. I know how much your mother and father would want to hear from you."

Before Mrs. Dewitt could say anything else, we heard commotion coming from the hallway. We both got up to see what was going on. It seemed a rush of bodyguards came out of nowhere, and they were all talking into their earpieces. The voices were overlapping each other so it was hard for me to decipher what was being said. The only thing I did manage to understand was when one burly man, who was a staggering six foot eight, woofed, "There's been a security breach!"

"What's going on?" I asked a rather calm Mrs. Dewitt.

"I don't know, but don't worry. This place is guarded probably better than the White House. Whoever breached the security will be reprimanded, trust me."

Just then, father and son came walking downstairs. I noticed both had guns. I had never seen Dalvin with a weapon before, and for the first time, it was really clicking that he was a gangsta.

"Baby, what's going on?" I asked Dalvin.

He kissed me on the cheek and continued to follow his father. Mrs. Dewitt didn't even bother asking her husband any questions. It was as if she knew now wasn't the time. I hadn't gotten to that comfort zone with Dalvin yet.

"Dear, let's go in the kitchen until we get further word of what is going on," Mrs. Dewitt said to me.

Curiosity had gotten the best of me, and I wanted to be knee-deep in the drama. There was no way I could patiently sit and wait to get word. I wanted to be at the world premiere, seeing all the footage before everybody else. I knew I couldn't say that to Mrs. Dewitt, so I reluctantly turned to go back in the kitchen. But then the doorbell rang, followed by a pounding on the door.

"I know my daughter's in there, now open this door!" I heard what sounded like my dad say.

Everybody turned and looked at me. Then, Dalvin Senior went to the door and opened it. My dad brushed passed him with what seemed like an army-deep of men who were more than capable of competing with his enemies. I was now standing in the corner, not wanting to be seen by my dad, but still able to peep at everything that was going on.

The second my dad brushed passed Dalvin's father, all the guards and my boyfriend raised their guns, ready to fire. Then, all my dad's bodyguards swarmed in front of him, raising their weapons. It was like the war in Iraq had found its way right here in the foyer of a mansion outside of Chicago.

"Everybody, calm down," Mrs. Dewitt announced as if she was an angel that was heaven-sent to stop the bloodbath that was about to go down. But no one lowered their guns. They all seemed frozen in the moment. "What, are you going to kill each other right here in my home?"

"I just want my daughter," my dad said, stepping through the shield of men trying to protect him.

"You're disrespecting my wife and family by

trespassing and barging into our home. If everyone in this house, including your daughter, dies because of that, weren't your actions all in vain?"

There was complete silence. It was like what Mr. Dewitt said was registering in my dad's brain. The ball was now in his court, and everyone was waiting to see what his next move would be.

"If that's the only way to get my daughter out this house, then so be it." Even with fingers one touch from pulling the trigger, my dad still spoke in his normal arrogant tongue.

"Daddy, will you stop!" I screamed, running from the corner where I felt protected, right to the center of the war. All the guns were still raised, and one mistake, I would no longer be standing, but instead on the floor surrounded by a puddle of my own blood.

"Mercedes, go back to the corner!" Dalvin demanded.

I saw the love and fear in his eyes as he stood there with his gun raised. He knew that it could go down at any moment and there wasn't anything he could do to stop it. I wanted to run to my boyfriend and feel his embrace, but this was going too far, and I had to do what I could to stop it.

"Daddy, I'll leave with you, but please have your men put their guns down. You can't come in here threatening Dalvin's family and expect to walk out alive. And what about me? Do you want me to die because of you? Let it go. I'm begging you, please don't do this."

My dad stood there staring at me for what seemed to be a lifetime. He then turned to the men and gestured for them to put down their guns. "Let's go, Mercedes," my dad said, calmly.

I walked over to Dalvin and gave him a long kiss.

"I love you."

"I love you too. You don't have to go."

"Yes, I do."

Dalvin didn't want to admit it, but he knew that if I didn't leave right now, then the consequences would be detrimental.

As I walked towards the front door, I stopped and looked at Dalvin's parents. "I'm sorry for all the confusion I caused in your home."

"It's not your fault, dear," Mrs. Dewitt replied as she reached out and handed me my purse.

Mr. Dewitt stopped my dad with a glare in his eyes. "Ronald, don't ever come to my home again." My dad just grabbed my arm and we walked out the door.

There was complete silence the whole ride home. I didn't know what to say to my dad. For the second day in a row, his actions made me ashamed of him. His behavior could've caused the death of everyone in that house, including mine. That couldn't be love. It was his ego taking what he felt belonged to him.

I was torn. I wanted to be with Dalvin more than anything in this world, but I couldn't help but wonder that as soon as the door shut, would his father begin contemplating the murder of my dad? I honestly couldn't blame him, but I didn't want anybody's blood on my hands. I assumed that my dad was plotting the same thing against Dalvin and his dad. If my dad killed Dalvin's father, then he would no doubt have to take out his son. Because if he didn't, Dalvin wouldn't stop until he got revenge for his dad's murderer.

When we finally got home, I went straight upstairs to my room and locked the door. I didn't want to see or speak to anybody. I heard my mother calling out my name when she realized I was back, but I ran past her, ignoring her pleas. My life was in complete chaos. I so desperately wanted to run off with Dalvin where no one could ever find us, but that was unrealistic.

Then I reflected on the conversation I had with Mrs. Dewitt and how she chose her husband over her father. I could honestly say that I wanted to do the same thing. The only difference was, her father was a judge, so she knew he wasn't going to commit murder to keep them apart. But my father showed me that he was more than willing to be a killer, and so was Dalvin's dad. That meant that neither one would back down.

As I got further and further into my thoughts, I heard my cell phone ringing. It was Dalvin. "Baby, hi."

"Are you okay?"

"No, I'm not. I want to cry my heart out, but I know it won't make a difference."

"Mercedes, don't. Baby, it will be alright."

"How? I can't believe I was in a house surrounded by guns where both of the men I love could've been killed."

"I know. I'm sorry you had to see that. But on the real, your pops didn't leave us a choice."

"I understand that. I really do. But where does it stop? If anything else happened because of me, I wouldn't be able to forgive myself. I love you so much, and I know what I have to do."

"What are you sayin', Mercedes?"

"As much as I love you, Dalvin, I have to let you go. My Dad isn't backing down, and if we keep seeing each other, somebody is goin' to end up dead. That's the truth. I don't want to destroy both of our lives and the lives of our families."

"Don't do this, Mercedes. We've been through too

much. We can get through this."

"How? Tell me how we can make this work without everything around us crumbling."

"I'll think of somethin'. But losing you isn't even up for debate. Baby, you mean the world to me. On everything I love, you gon' be my wife one day, don't you understand that?"

My heart was aching to the point that I felt like I might not be able to breathe much longer. Knowing that Dalvin truly loved me and really wanted to make me his wife was all I needed to survive in this world. But having that love meant guaranteeing our death. Because if we were together and my dad had Dalvin killed, then I would no doubt die of a broken heart.

"Baby, I do understand that, and that's why I have to let you go. It's killing me to even say these words, but there's no other way." I wanted to express more of my feelings to him, but the persistent knock at the door wouldn't stop. "Whoever that is, will you please go away! I don't feel like talkin'."

"Mercedes, it's your mother, and I need to speak to you." She stressed the word "need" and I knew I couldn't avoid her forever.

"Give me a minute," I said, sucking my teeth. "Baby, let me call you back. My mother's about to break down the door, so let me see what she wants."

"Make sure you call me back."

"I will. I promise."

"I love you."

"I love you too, Dalvin." I did love him, and that's why all this unnecessary drama was killing me.

After closing my phone shut and getting carried away with my thoughts, I finally got off the bed, and with hesitation, opened my door. I immediately turned my back and walked back over to my bed. All these recent mother and daughter conversations taking place in my bedroom were getting on my last nerves.

"I don't want to lose you," were the first words that came out my mother's mouth. I still remained quiet, not knowing how to respond to that, so I didn't. "You're my daughter and my only child. I want you in my life." Her voice had the echoes of pleas, as if she knew I was almost gone. I guess a mother does know her child, because mentally, I was one step away from being devoid of my parents.

"Then convince Daddy to let me be with Dalvin," I stated, staring her directly in her face. I knew I was asking the impossible, but I wanted to know if she was even willing to try.

"Believe it or not, Mercedes, I've tried. Yesterday when you ran out of here, I begged your father all day and night to let you follow your heart and be with Dalvin. But he doesn't listen to me, and honestly, he doesn't care what I think." My mother put her head down as if ashamed. When she looked back up, the tears were engulfing her eyes. "I know you think I'm weak and hate the way I don't stand up to your father, and I'm sorry for being such a disappointment. But I'm not like you, Mercedes. I don't have your strength and determination. I know a mother is supposed to protect her child and be strong, but I'm still growing up myself. Please forgive me for not being a better mother."

My mother's lips were quivering and her hands were shaking. My heart went out to her. She was still stuck in being that naïve fifteen year old my dad met years ago. She never broke out of that shell, and I sympathized with that. I ran over and gave her a long hug. "You're a good mother," I whispered in her ear.

It was easy for me to forget that all my mother had was my dad. He had been the center of her world for so long. Yes, she did have me, but she still raised me based on my dad's rules. He regulated everything and everyone in his life.

"You don't hate me?"

"Ma, of course I don't hate you. I was so caught up in my pain I didn't realize you were hurtin' too."

"Mercedes, I will do everything I can to try and convince your dad to let you be with Dalvin, but I'm not sure it will help." My mother was being honest, and I appreciated that.

"I've decided not to see Dalvin anymore." Hearing myself say that to someone gave me a lump in my throat.

"What?" It was obvious my mother was shocked by what I said. "I don't understand."

"Ma, I can't take it anymore. There was about to be an all out war in Dalvin's house today. Daddy wouldn't back down. He came there armed, and of course, Dalvin's people were ready for war too. I can't do this. I love Dalvin so much, and if I could, I'd run off and marry him tomorrow. But I know our being together is just gonna cause bloodshed, and I don't want to be responsible for that."

"Oh, my little girl, I know how hard this must be for you. I'm so sorry. You don't deserve this life."

"Neither do you," I stated. "How can you stand to be married to a man so cruel? He doesn't care about how other people feel, or how his decisions can destroy so many lives. He's stuck on gettin' what he wants, and that's all he cares about. First, he tried to practically shake me to death, then he came to my boyfriend's home with some type of death wish. I can't believe I never knew what a monster he was."

"Mercedes, stop. Your dad is wrong, but he does love you."

"Yeah, he loves me when I'm his perfect little daughter, doin' what makes him happy. That's not love. That's him wanting to control me. He's ruining my life, and I'll never forgive him for that."

"Say what?" my dad asked as he came walking through the door. My head actually started hurting when I saw his face.

"Nothing. Mercedes and I were talking about some things," my mother explained, trying to play peacemaker.

But I wasn't having it. I wanted my dad to know exactly what I felt. "No, he needs to know," I said, looking at my mother as her eyes implored me to let it go. "I'm not goin' to see Dalvin anymore."

"Mercedes, I'm so proud of you. I knew you'd come around." My dad reached over to hug me and I pulled away.

"Don't touch me!" The joyous look my dad had on his face a minute ago had now faded. "I'm not leaving Dalvin because I love you so much, it's because of my love for him. I realized today that you're a heartless monster, and you'll never let me be happy with him. Because of your determination to have it your way, somebody will die if Dalvin and I stay together, and I wouldn't be able to live with myself knowing that. So you've won, but in the process, you've lost me."

"Baby girl, I know you might be upset with me right now, but one day you'll realize I've done this for your own good. You would have nothing but heartbreak being with a boy like Dalvin."

"He couldn't break my heart no more than what you've been doin' these past few days. I wish I wasn't your daughter," I said slowly, so every word would resonate.

"I expect for you to keep your word and never see Dalvin again," he said, before turning around and walking out the door and out my life as far as I was concerned.

$\mathscr{C}$hapter 9

Twisted

It had been over three weeks since I'd spoken to Dalvin, and over a month since I saw him before walking out of his door with my dad. If I had known the kiss I gave him was going to be the last one, I would've made it much longer.

After having it out with my parents, and they left my room, feeling heartbroken, I called Dalvin and officially ended it. For the next week he called me nonstop, telling me he couldn't let me walk out of his life, but I knew I had no choice. I finally changed my cell number so he couldn't get in touch with me. I purposely stayed in the house for the next few weeks so I wouldn't run into him. I knew my heart was too weak, and if I saw him, he would pull me right back in.

But now it was time for me to get out and get some fresh air. I was tired of being cooped up in the house in my room. I rarely went downstairs, only for meals, and I would bring them back upstairs to my bedroom.

Keisha started complaining that I was ruining her summer and threatened to go back to New York if I didn't snap out of my funk. I didn't want that to happen, since she was the only person that I really had to talk to.

"Are you ready yet?" Keisha smacked as I was

dabbing on some lip gloss.

"Girl, calm down. Let me get my purse and we out."

"Good, because I'm so happy we're gettin' out this house. I was startin' to feel like I was in a prison camp."

I rolled my eyes at her, because she always had to exaggerate the facts.

I grabbed my keys and headed downstairs. "Ma, we're about to go to the fair they're havin' at Millennium Park."

"I'm so happy the two of you are getting out this house." My mother was smiling, happy to see me out of my sweats and T-shirt and in some cute clothes.

"Me too," my dad chimed in. I still wasn't speaking to him, but he would always try to make a friendly comment to me on the rare occasions the opportunity presented itself.

"Thanks," I said flatly. "Let's go, Keisha. I know you gettin' antsy."

It felt weird when I got in my car. I hadn't driven it since I had escaped to Dalvin's house that day. When my dad came to get me, he had one of his bodyguards drive it back home. But after putting the top down and blasting The Breakthrough, by my girl, Mary J. Blige, I felt right back at home.

When we pulled up to the park, the fair was already jumping. The parking lot was full, and I instantly zoomed in on all the happy couples holding hands. I had to stop the tears that were sneaking up on me. Dalvin and I were supposed to be here, holding hands and in love.

"Let it go. Don't even think about it," Keisha said as she caught me eyeing one couple in particular for a long time. They were a very attractive couple, around the same age as Dalvin and me.

"That's easier said than done."

"Mercedes, we're supposed to be out having a good time."

"You're right. Let me snap out my funk."

For the next couple of hours, Keisha and I rode every ride as we bribed people with either money or flirting so we could cut to the front of the line. After getting off the pirate ship, we were ready to stuff our faces. We were both dying for the famous barbecue ribs they served every year. On our way to get something to eat, we laughed and joked about the one boy that vomited as soon as he got off the ride.

We both stopped in our tracks when we saw the two couples walking towards us.

"Girl, ignore it and let's just keep walkin'," Keisha said, casually grabbing my hand to keep me on the path.

I so badly wanted to show out, but I knew she was right. I didn't even make eye contact. I continued to walk straight ahead as if on a mission. Once I knew we had passed them, I let out a deep sigh of relief, until I felt the familiar touch of a hand on my shoulder.

"What, you thought I was gonna just let you walk past me and not say nothin'?"

"What is there to say?"

"You changed your cell number. I haven't spoken to you in weeks, and you gon' ask me what is there to say?"

"You seem to be doin' just fine, Dalvin," I said, glancing over at the cute little petite girl I assumed was his date. The other girl was holding hands with some guy I had never seen Dalvin with before.

"How could you just cut me off like that?"

"Does it matter? You've obviously moved on. I knew you wasn't goin' to be sitting around missing me forever, but you've moved on pretty quickly if I say so myself."

"You left me, remember?" Dalvin reminded me. "I haven't stopped missing you... never will." He reached his hand out to me, and that's when Keisha intervened.

"Come on, Mercedes, it's time to go." She knew I was about to surrender to my feelings.

"Why don't you stay out of this? This ain't got nothin' to do wit' you. This between me and Mercedes."

"Listen, D, I'm tryna protect my cousin."

"She don't need protection from me."

"Dalvin, I really need to go. Besides, your friend seems to be gettin' anxious. You don't want to keep her waiting."

"This ain't about her, this about us."

"There is no 'us'."

Dalvin gave me a strange look before speaking. "Yo, was you gamin' me? Did you ever love me, or was I just some excitement for you to rile up your daddy? Better yet, was I even your first, or did you pretend to be a virgin to get me further caught up in you? Yeah, that's right, you pretended to be a virgin, just like you pretended to be in love wit' me."

"Will you stop it?" I felt like the walls were closing in on me. I was so stunned by Dalvin's accusations that I couldn't even put my thoughts together to defend his allegations.

"You not denying it. Yo, you just a worthless trick," he continued, pointing his finger in my face. "I wanna smack you down to the ground like the trash you are, but you're not even worth it."

I could no longer contain my composure and broke down crying.

"D, that's enough!" Keisha said, coming to my defense.

"Don't worry about it, I'm done here. Save those fake tears for someone who cares."

My sobs became louder, as if they were begging Dalvin to come back. But when he turned his back on me and walked away, it was his way of saying goodbye forever.

"Mercedes, come sit down."

The tears wouldn't stop flowing, and thank goodness I had Keisha with me, although there was nothing she could say to stop the stinging pain my heart was in. Keisha went and got some napkins to wipe away my tears, but that still wouldn't wipe the words Dalvin said to me out of my mind.

"I can't believe he said those things to me. Doesn't he know how much I love him?"

"Mercedes, he didn't mean it. He's just hurt and wanted to hurt you too."

I knew Keisha was right. Dalvin felt that I rejected him, and it turned him cold towards me. But I did love him, that's why I let him go. Now he hated me, and I didn't know which one hurt more; letting him go, or knowing that he detested me.

"Keisha, I never knew love could hurt so bad. I don't ever want to feel this type of pain again."

"It gets easier, trust me. I remember the first time my heart was broken. I thought I would never date another boy again, but eventually I got over it, and so will you."

"But I don't want to get over Dalvin, and I know this will sound selfish, but I don't want him to get over me either."

"That's not selfish, it's called being in love. But, Mercedes, letting D go was the right thing to do for both of y'all. Things had gotten way too crazy, and it was only gonna get worse. D's pride is hurt right now, but one day he'll understand why you did what you did."

I wanted to believe Keisha, but my feeling of despair was still there. I looked back up in the direction I last saw Dalvin, hoping that he would be coming back to me, saying how sorry he was, but he wasn't there. He was gone, and part of me hoped that I would never see him again, because it was too painful knowing that we could never be together again.

After pulling it together, Keisha and I finally did eat some barbecue ribs, and then we left the fair.

"Girl, let me get off at this exit, because my gas tank is almost empty. With all the frustrations I had today, I don't need to get stuck on this highway."

"Yeah, 'cause it's too hot out here to be pushing your car, and too dangerous to be hitchhiking for a ride."

We both burst out laughing, knowing neither of us would do any of the above.

"I'm so happy we made it to the gas station. I was worried for a minute. I can't believe I was doin' all that driving on basically an empty tank." I pulled up to the full service pump and waited for a service man. After handing him my credit card, I wanted to stop in the store and get a candy bar. "Do you want anything from the store?" I asked Keisha.

"Naw, I'm still full from them barbecue ribs we had. I can't believe you about to stuff your mouth again."

"I know, right? But I'm still hungry." I went in the store, grabbed a candy bar and a few other goodies. When I came out, I noticed a silver 650i coupe had pulled up to the passenger side of my car. The dude was talking to Keisha, and as I approached, he looked familiar to me, but I couldn't remember from where.

Deja King

"Hi, Mercedes. Your cousin was keeping me company while I was waiting for you."

"Waiting for me? Do I know you?"

"I met you a couple of months back at the mall." He could tell I was still trying to place his face. "You dropped your keys and I picked them up, then your boyfriend walked up."

"Oh, now I remember. How are you?"

"Better, now that Keisha told me you're single again." Keisha gave me a devious smile.

"I see. What was your name again?" I got back in the car, somewhat annoyed that Keisha was obviously trying to play matchmaker.

"Jacob. You should let me take you out to dinner or something. I promise we'll have a good time."

"I don't know. I'm not really up to dating yet."

"D obviously is, so maybe you need to make yourself ready," Keisha said.

I knew Keisha wasn't trying to stab me with her words, but they still hurt. Dalvin was moving on, and I needed to start too. I only had a few weeks left before it would be time for me to go back to school. I could either spend them moping around thinking about Dalvin, or trying to have some fun.

"So, what do you say, Mercedes? Are you going to give me a chance?"

"Sure, why not."

"That's what's up! How about I take you out to dinner tomorrow night?"

I wasn't planning on going out with him so soon, but I guess there was no sense in waiting. I gave Jacob my number and he drove off.

"I'm so glad you goin' out with Jacob. He seems

108

cool, and it's a must that you get D off your mind."

"I doubt anybody can do that, but it's worth a try."

That night when I went to bed, I tossed and turned all night. At least three different times I wanted to pick up the phone, call Dalvin and profess my undying love for him, but something held me back. If I went there with him, then I would have to be ready to fight the war all over again, and that was out of the question. So, instead of calling him, I reached under my mattress and got the picture that I kept hidden of him, and fell asleep with it next to my heart.

Chapter 10

P.S. I'm Still Not Over You

As the day progressed, I started to dread my upcoming date with Jacob. There didn't seem to be anything wrong with him, he just wasn't Dalvin. When he called earlier to get my address, I started to cancel on him right then, but Keisha gave me a foul look so I kept the date.

"So, Keisha tells me you're going on a date tonight." I could tell by my mother's tone that she was excited about the news. She desperately wanted me to break out of my funk, and I'm sure she hoped this new guy would do just that.

"Yeah, but it's no big deal. We're only goin' out to dinner."

"That's a start. I'm proud of you."

I was about to confess to her that going out on this date was a mistake because my heart belonged to Dalvin, but then my dad came into the kitchen and I went mute.

"Ronny, Mercedes is going on a date tonight with a young man named Jacob. Isn't that wonderful?"

"Yes, it is, but I need to meet him first."

"Is that really necessary?" my mother asked, hoping my father wouldn't cause any more drama.

"It's okay, Ma, Dad can meet him."

"Of course it's okay, Toy," he remarked sarcastically.

"What time is he coming to pick you up?"

"Around seven."

"I'll be here then."

"I'm sure you will."

But honestly, I did want my dad to be here. I wanted him to grill Jacob unmercifully so that he'd crack under the pressure, and my dad would forbid me to go out on a date with him. Or, I wanted Jacob to get so turned off by my dad's obvious over the top arrogance that he'd walk out the door and never come back. Either way, I wouldn't have to go out on a date with him, which was the resolution I was hoping for.

After dragging my feet, I finally went upstairs to start getting ready for what I hoped to be a date that never happened. When I got in the shower, I lathered my body with soap, reminiscing about the time Dalvin and I made love. Realizing that I would never feel his embrace made me appreciate the memory that much more.

I let the water drench me for a little while longer before stepping out the shower. I checked the time, and realized that Jacob would be showing up any minute. But it was my plan to still be getting dressed when he arrived so it would give my dad more time to shred him to pieces.

As I lotioned my body, I heard my cousin's big mouth. "Mercedes, you need to hurry up! Jacob's here!"

"Dang, I'm comin'!"

"What's takin you so long anyway? You know Uncle Ronny's gonna be giving him the third degree. Hurry up before he scares Jacob off."

If Keisha only knew that's what I was praying for. "If you keep running your mouth, I'll never get dressed. Go back downstairs and I'll be down in a few."

"Fine, I'm goin' downstairs, but you need to hurry

up," she hissed.

I began brushing my hair back in a ponytail, thinking that I should be getting dressed for a date with Dalvin, not Jacob. I was at the point that I couldn't stand my parents or Keisha for pressuring me to go on this sorry date. All I yearned to do was cuddle up next to Dalvin and steal kisses between eating popcorn while at the movie theater, but now that was nothing but a wish.

By the time I finished getting dressed, it was twenty minutes later, and Keisha had come upstairs three more times. I took my time walking down the stairs, tuning my ears for any raised angry voices, but to my utter disgust, all I heard was laughter.

"Hi, everybody," I said, greeting the room with a fake, cheerful smile.

"We're glad you finally managed to grace us with your presence." Of course my dad had to be the first to make a sarcastic remark.

"But you were worth the wait. You look beautiful," Jacob commented as he handed me a bouquet of stunning flowers.

My parents and Keisha was eating it up. It was obvious they were all feeling him. I had to admit the flowers were a nice gesture, and he looked very handsome and clean cut in his slacks and button up shirt, in direct contrast to the sleek, rap superstar attire Dalvin wore so well.

"Thank you. The flowers are beautiful."

"I'll take those for you, honey, and put them in some water."

"I appreciate that, Ma."

"Well, we should really get going. We're already late for our reservations at Charlie Trotter's."

"Very impressive. You two have a great evening."

I couldn't believe how supportive my dad was being. Boy, oh boy, did Jacob have his game tight. To win my dad over was no small feat, and he had him almost pushing us down the altar.

"Thank you, sir. It was a pleasure meeting you all. I won't have your daughter out too late."

"Don't worry about it, she's in great hands." My dad gave me a kiss on the forehead, and the whole Jacob cheerleading squad waved goodbye as we departed. Jacob opened the door for me to his car, and we headed off.

When we reached Charlie Trotter's, it was packed. Charlie Trotter's was one of the most renowned fine dining establishments in Chicago. Although we were almost an hour late for our reservations, the hostess gladly sat us at a prime table, going so far as to call Jacob by his first name.

"You must be a regular here."

"Yes, I come here frequently with my father."

"I never asked how old you were."

"About to turn nineteen."

"Oh, so do you work for your dad, or are you in school?" I had already decided to bombard Jacob with questions. I was curious to find out what my dad found so special about him. Why did he give his blessings to this guy, and find him so much more suitable than the man I truly loved?

"I don't work for my dad yet. He's actually a very successful investment banker. I'm about to start my second year at Duke University."

"Wow, you attend the same school as the lacrosse team rapists! Are they friends of yours?"

"No!" he answered smugly. "But what happened to innocent until proven guilty?"

"Silly me! White men, black woman. It seems from the beginning of time, white men have been tryin' to make black women their sex slaves. I guess it's biased of me to just assume the alleged victim is telling the truth."

"Rape cases are always a difficult thing, and honestly, I don't know any of the parties involved. But hopefully justice will be served." Jacob was obviously riding on the fence, because he was giving me no clue as to what side he was on. "But enough talk about that. Let's talk about you."

"What about me?"

"What happened between you and your very protective boyfriend?"

"Things didn't work out between us." With him just bringing up Dalvin, I found myself getting hot and flustered. His question seemed innocent enough, but the wound from the break up hadn't even begun to heal yet.

"How could things not work out with someone as special as you? You're the type of girl that once a guy has the opportunity to have you in their life, they never let you go."

"Sometimes life isn't fair, especially when it comes to love."

"Love! So you were in love?"

Thank goodness the waitress came to our table to take our order, because I was in no mood to answer Jacob's question. He was trying to enter off limits territory, and if he kept pushing, he was going to push me right away before the date even started.

After ordering my food, I excused myself to go to the ladies room. I needed a moment to calm my nerves. I was moving too fast trying to get over Dalvin. I had been in mourning for a month, but I think I needed at least a month more.

When I entered the bathroom, I was thrilled that it was empty. I sat on the stool in front of the vanity mirror. I wanted to see if the pain in my heart was reflected anywhere on my face. They say the eyes never lie, and from the look in mine, I had to agree with that statement. It seemed apparent that I had either lost my best friend, a cherished family pet, or the love of my life. I would say two out of three, which meant I was wearing double the toll.

I looked at my watch and realized I had been sitting in the mirror almost fifteen minutes. I was surprised that Jacob didn't come looking to make sure I hadn't fell in the toilet, or better yet, made a quick exit out the back door. I stood up, gathered my bearings and headed out.

"Excuse you!" the girl smacked as I accidentally bumped her going out the door.

"I apologize. I wasn't paying attention."

"That's obvious. So watch yourself the next time."

Now I paused and studied the girl, because her attitude was a bit too obnoxiously hoochie for an establishment like this. She did look familiar, but I couldn't place her face.

"I apologized. Don't take it overboard. It's not that deep. Don't act like nobody ain't neva accidentally bumped you before." I could get just as hoochie as any other chick.

"Whatever! I ain't got time to go back and forth wit you, my man's waiting for me, so excuse you!"

That chick was rubbing me the wrong way, and I was ready to go toe to toe with her, but I knew this wasn't the time or place for a brawl. Plus, I wasn't even a fighter, but with the bad funk I was in, I felt I could beat down almost anybody. I let the girl pass me by and headed back to my table.

"I was getting worried about you," Jacob commented as I sat down.

"My cousin, Keisha called me while I was in the bathroom. I was in the hall listening to her ask me a million and one questions."

"Oh, she wanted to see how our date was going?" he smiled, feeling important.

"Yeah, she was yapping on and on about you."

"I hope you told her we were having a nice time."

"Of course I did."

As Jacob went on talking, I noticed the girl I had the minor altercation with in the bathroom was walking towards her table. I was curious to see what man Miss Thing was rushing to get back to. They were sitting at a corner table, and the guy's back was turned away from me, so I couldn't see his face.

"Mercedes, are you there?" Jacob questioned, waving his hand in front of my face like he was trying to snap me out of a hypnotic trance.

"I'm sorry, Jacob. I didn't get a lot of sleep last night and I was drifting off."

"I think it's something else. You miss your ex-boyfriend. It's understandable."

His attitude caught me off guard. He was a good looking guy with a lot going for himself, and I figured his ego would be offended that I was stuck on another man, but he seemed to be a lot more reasonable than I was giving him credit for.

"You're right, I am thinking about Dalvin." I decided not to lie. If we had any chance of building a relationship, being honest was a good place to start.

"I figured that, but I appreciate you being honest about it."

"Jacob, if I could really be honest, I didn't even want to go on this date. I was hoping my tyrant of a father would hate you and forbid me to see you like he did with Dalvin. Unfortunately, it didn't work out like that. Now, here we are, and I wish it was Dalvin that was sittin' in your seat." Many would say that I gave Jacob way too much information, and I probably did. I knew he was going to curse me out and leave me sitting here all alone, with me having to call my daddy for a ride home.

Jacob took a deep breath and tapped his fingers on the table. He then picked up his glass of water, and for a minute, I thought he was going to toss his water in my face. He would have every right to, but there would be a major problem if he did cross that line.

"Mercedes, was Dalvin your first boyfriend?"

"Yeah, why?"

"Losing someone you love is always hard the first time. It may take you a month, a year or ten years to get over it, but I promise you, eventually life does go on. You may not want it to go on with me, but I'd love it if you at least gave me a chance."

"You're not mad at what I just told you?"

"Mad, no. Disappointed, yes. It's not easy to hear a young lady you're interested in tell you she'd rather be on a date with someone else. But I love a challenge. Like I said, if you give me a chance, I welcome the opportunity to show you that you can be happier with me than you ever were with Dalvin."

I seriously doubted that Jacob could ever make me happier than Dalvin, but because he was being so cool about the whole situation, I wanted to give him the opportunity to prove me wrong.

For the next hour, Jacob and I ate, laughed and had a wonderful conversation. He was educated on a long list of topics, so not only did he hold my attention, I was also very intrigued by him. He reminded me of a black hip version of the white boys I went to prep school with. He didn't have the street edge that made Dalvin so appealing, but Jacob had his own aura, which made him shine.

"So, are you ready to get out of here?"

"Yeah. I really enjoyed myself, Jacob. Thank you."

"It was my pleasure."

After paying the bill, Jacob and I headed out.

"I have to bring Keisha here. The food was off the chain."

"She'll enjoy that. My dad and I can't get enough of this place."

"Excuse me, sir," we heard someone scream out as the door was closing behind us. We both turned around and saw our waitress flagging her hand. We both walked in as she ran up. "You forgot your credit card."

"Thank you. Don't want to leave without this."

As the waitress handed Jacob his credit card, I first noticed the belligerent girl from the bathroom coming towards us, and then I felt myself about to vomit when her date appeared right behind her. Her familiar face was no longer a mystery.

"Baby, that's the silly chick I was tellin' you about from the bathroom," she sniped to her man as she brushed past me.

Jacob paused and stared at the girl as he heard what she said. I'm sure the whole restaurant heard her as she was severely lacking in discretion.

At that moment, her man and I made eye contact. He

met me with the same cold stare that I saw the last time we crossed paths.

"Is there a problem?" Jacob asked, taking my hand. He was coming to save the day. But then he quickly recognized the familiar face.

"Who are you, and why are you grabbing on my girl's hand?" Right after Dalvin let the words slip out of his mouth he caught himself, but it was too late.

"Your girl? I'm your girl!" hoochie mama spat as she stepped closer to Dalvin. Then she gave me a from the floor to the ceiling stare. "Oh, you that chick, Mercedes that we saw the other day at the fair. That's why you bumped me when you was staggering out the bathroom."

"Sweetheart, that was an accident. Ain't nobody checkin' for you like that. And I wasn't staggering, so chill wit' the dramatics."

"Everybody needs to calm down," Jacob said.

"Yo, son, this ain't got nothing to do wit' you. And you still didn't answer my question. Why you holding her hand?"

"Because Mercedes is my date, and I don't appreciate your girl approaching her in that manner."

"I didn't approach her, I simply stated the facts. Her silly butt bumped me on the way out the bathroom, and I believe she did that mess on purpose."

"Yo, Sholanda, shut the hell up!" Dalvin barked, and like a good dog, she did just that.

"You on a date wit' this dude?"

I felt myself about to melt right there. Dalvin was looking so sexy in his off-white linen shorts and shirt to match. The thick diamond bracelet and diamond rope chain he was sporting had me thinking we were supposed to be on a video set instead of in a supercilious restaurant. Instead of lashing out at me with his tongue, I wanted it down my throat. While daydreaming, I felt Jacob squeezing my hand, letting me know to answer Dalvin's question.

"Ah, yeah, sorta."

"Yeah, she's on a date wit' that dude, baby. She's already moved on. She ain't worth your time, Dalvin."

I yanked my hand out of Jacob's grasp. I was about to give my best shot and club the hoochie.

"Yo, didn't I tell you to shut up!" Dalvin was becoming flustered. He was really pissed at me, but because Sholanda kept putting her two cents in, he was screaming on her. Then he looked back at Jacob. His eyes seemed to just zoom in on him. "I don't ever forget a face. Ain't this that clown that was steppin' to you at the mall way back, even after you told him you had a man?"

"Yeah, I'm that man. But since you couldn't hold on to her, I stepped in."

The specks of green that would spark in Dalvin's hazel eyes when he was on the verge of exploding were now flashing. I saw him balling his fists, and I stepped in between him and Jacob.

"Move, Mercedes." Dalvin said in that calm before the storm voice.

"Dalvin, don't do this. Jacob didn't mean what he said."

"You don't have to speak up for me, Mercedes. I'm very capable of defending myself."

"You heard him. He'll handle this whooping I'm 'bout to put on him like a real man would. Now move out the way, Mercedes."

"I know you ain't about to fight up in here over this trick!"

That was all I could stand. It was like I couldn't control myself. My fists started flying as if someone else was powering them. I think Shalonda was as shocked as I was, because all she could do was bend her head down and put her hands up, trying to protect her face. I turned into a deranged crazy person. I stopped swinging punches and got a strong grip on her hair. I held it tightly, knocked her hands out of the way and just started smacking her across the face like how parents whip their kids on their butts. Her eyes had the most pleading look of fear, shock and disbelief. But what did she expect? Her petite little self shouldn't have been yapping on like she was Laila Ali. The way she was carrying on with that mouth, I thought she was one of those tiny girls that could fight their butts off. But instead, she turned out to be like those little puppies whose bark is bigger than their bite.

"Get this crazy girl off me!" Sholanda finally managed to say between smacks.

That's when both Dalvin and Jacob grabbed me at the same time, as if I needed both their help to get me off her. While they had my arms pinned behind my back, the slick trick sneaked in a sucker slap. "Now what? Now what?" she started hissing.

"Let me go! I'ma kill that hoochie!" I was livid. I couldn't believe the little punk waited until I was jammed up to sneak in a chump shot.

Just when Sholanda was coming back at me again for part two, Dalvin grabbed her by the throat. "Shalonda, that's enough!"

"Come on, Mercedes, we need to get out of here."

People started gathering around, wondering what was going on.

When Dalvin let Sholanda go, she went right back

to running her mouth. "When I catch you on them streets, I'ma get you!"

"What street is that? Me and you, we don't be on the same streets, sweetheart. Dalvin, you need to drop her back off at whatever dog pound you found her at. She obviously didn't get her rabies shot!"

Sholanda had the nerve to try to jump at me like she wanted some more of me, knowing that Dalvin was going to stop her anyway.

I turned and walked away as Jacob followed behind me. I was steaming. I felt like blowing up the entire place just to guarantee that I wiped Sholanda off the earth.

"Are you okay, Mercedes?"

"What do you think?" I snapped.

"I know you're upset, but try to calm down."

I knew this wasn't Jacob's fault, but since I couldn't go upside Sholanda's head, he was the next best thing. "Take me home, please."

There was complete silence during the entire ride, and by the time we arrived at my house, my anger had begun to subside.

"I know things ended on a bad note, but up until that point, I enjoyed our date." I looked at Jacob and couldn't help but smile.

"It did get a little messy, but to my surprise, I enjoyed myself too. If you're up to it, I'd like to take you out again."

"You mean my behavior didn't scare you off?"

"No. On the real, I was ready to shut Sholanda up too." We both started laughing.

"I'm sorry I hesitated tellin' Dalvin we were on a date. That couldn't of felt too good."

"Luckily, you had already expressed your feelings

about him to me, so I wasn't surprised you held back. I don't care what Dalvin thinks anyway. I'm only concerned about how you feel about me."

"Well, I'd love to go on another date with you."

"Great! I'll call you tomorrow. Now let me walk you to the door."

"You don't have to do that."

"Yes, I do. A lady deserves to be treated as such." Jacob came around to my door and opened it for me. When we got to my door, he gave me a kiss on the cheek and left. I had to admit that he was an amazing date.

"I'm home!" I screamed, knowing that my parents and Keisha were waiting up to see how my date went. As I expected, all three came from the living room area as if I had been the topic of conversation all night.

"You're home so soon?" my dad was the first to ask.

"Yeah, we decided to end things early. But I had a great time."

"Really!" my mother said, sounding stunned, but thrilled.

"Jacob is a pretty cool guy. We're goin' on another date."

My dad smiled at my mother, as if telling her he knew I would get over Dalvin sooner than she thought. But boy was he wrong. I missed Dalvin so much that it was killing me inside. Because Jacob was so understanding and being patient with me, his company helped it not to hurt so bad.

"I'm happy to hear that, baby girl. I'm proud of you."

"Thanks, Daddy. I would love to stand here and discuss my evening, but I'm beat."

"That's fine, honey. Get some rest. You can tell me

about your date tomorrow."

"I will, Ma. Goodnight everybody."

By the time I was halfway up the stairs, I heard Keisha running trying to catch up with me. "You can duck your parents if you want to, but I want all the details."

"Of course you do, 'cause you nosy."

"That, and front if you like, but I know you dyin' to tell me what happened. You can't hold back."

I sucked my teeth because Keisha was right. She was my right hand, and I had to share the craziness of the evening with her.

When we entered my room, I shut and locked the door. I immediately started giving her a play by play of the night's events. Keisha sat there dumbfounded, listening to my story. She didn't even interrupt me until I was completely finished, which is unheard of for her. I finally had to tell her I was done after she was silent a little too long.

She sat shaking her head before speaking. "I don't know if I'm more shocked that you acted as if you bought the Floyd Mayweather confidence tape and became a boxer overnight, or you and D carrying on like y'all still go together."

"Two people don't get over each other overnight, it takes time."

"It's been over a month."

"You must ain't neva been in love, 'cause a month only feels like an hour when your heart belongs to someone. That pain stays fresh."

"I feel you, but y'all need to pull it together. You tryna fight all in the restaurant wit' D's new girl, and he tryna go at Jacob, all while he wit' the next chick. What type of sense does any of that make?"

"Love don't make sense, Keisha. You ain't neva heard that saying, 'Love will make a fool out of you'?"

"All I know is that you can have a potentially great relationship with Jacob, one that don't involve a shootout between families. So, instead of having brawls wit' D's new girl, you should let it go and move on."

Keisha proceeded to turn up the volume on the radio and started snapping her fingers to Mary J's, Enough Cryin'. "This is my part right here, Brooklyn!" she hollered before she started rhyming over Mary's rap verse.

"Enough already, Keisha! I don't need you to break out into a bad Mary imitation to get me to understand your point. I know it's time for me to forget about Dalvin, and I plan on doin' just that."

"That's my girl!" Keisha winked her eye and gave me a pound, as if she had accomplished the ultimate feat.

I did plan on forgetting about Dalvin, but it would be later rather than sooner. It seemed so easy to fall in love, but why was it so difficult to fall out of it?

Chapter 11

Someone To Watch Over Me

Like Jacob said he would, he called me the next, day and the day after that. As a matter of fact, he called me a few times just about everyday. We were spending a lot of time together, and although I enjoyed his company, Dalvin remained fixed in my mind. For whatever reason, I saw Jacob as more of a friend than anything else, but they say the best relationships start off as friendships.

"Let me guess. You're getting dressed for another date with Jacob," Keisha grinned.

"You know it. We're both leaving to go back to school soon, so he wants us to spend as much time together as possible."

"Can you believe the summer is winding down already? I feel like I just got here yesterday. I miss you already, Mercedes."

"Girl, I miss you too. At least you're goin' back to a school where your classmates have flavor. I have to go back to my dull prep school. I'm so sick of that place."

"I thought you were goin' to talk to your parents about transferring to a school closer to home."

"I was considering it, but with all the drama that took place this summer, it never seemed to be the right time. Plus, now that it's over between Dalvin and me, it's not as important. Being closer to him was a huge motivation. I no longer have that."

"So, you really let it go with Dalvin? I know how hard that was for you. You haven't spoken to him since y'all's fiasco at the restaurant?"

"No. I wanted to call him, but decided it was a bad idea. And of course, he doesn't have my new cell number. But even if he did, he probably wouldn't have called me."

"It's for the best anyway."

"Sounds good, but letting go is never easy."

"I feel you. So, where you and Jacob going?"

I knew Keisha was trying to change the subject away from Dalvin, so I eased on to the next topic. "Probably to the movies or something. I still haven't seen the new X-Men movie. I gotta see my girl, Halle Berry kick butt on the big screen."

"Yeah, I'm sure that joint is tight."

"You know what I meant to ask you?"

"What?

"Do you ever talk to Demetrius?" I knew we were supposed to have moved on with any matters regarding Dalvin, but I couldn't help myself.

"We speak once in awhile, but after you and D broke up, we both agreed that it would be too much of a conflict to keep kicking it."

"I'm sorry, Keisha. I know that you was feelin' him."

"Girl, if I was feelin' him to that point, I would've found a way to maintain that," she explained while laughing.

"I know your fast tail would've."

"You know I got a boyfriend back in NYC anyway, so my summer flings are just that."

"Does your boyfriend know that?"

"He betta, 'cause when I get home, all those other tricks he been kickin' it wit' while I was MIA betta crawl right back into they hole."

"You're too much!"

My cell phone started ringing as I was putting on my shoes. "That must be Jacob telling me he's here. "Hello."

"I'm out front."

"Okay, I'll be down in a couple of minutes. Girl, let me hurry up. I can't ever be on time."

"I hope you really take things to the next level with Jacob. He's a lot better for you than D. That street life needs to stay out there," Keisha said, pointing out the window. "Jacob's got his mind right, that's what you need."

"Maybe you're right. I'll consider giving Jacob a kiss tonight, and hopefully I'll see stars."

"Out of all the dates y'all been on, you still ain't kissed that boy?"

"Nope. And thank goodness he hasn't put any pressure on me."

"See, I knew he was the one for you. Any other guy would've kicked you to the curb by now. Y'all been goin' out just about every night for the last three weeks, and you ain't even give him no sugar?"

"Sugar? Girl, you're using grown folks language."

"And what? Sugar is sweet and everybody likes the taste of a little sugar."

"I'll let you know tonight if Jacob likes the taste of mine," I remarked as I headed out the door to meet him.

"You look beautiful," Jacob commented as I got in his car.

"Thanks. I was in the mood to put on a dress tonight."

"It's fitting every curve perfectly."

I did a quick double take at Jacob, because even

though I knew he was attracted to me, that was the first time he'd ever made such a blatant statement. I felt a bit uncomfortable, but shrugged it off.

"So, where are we going?"

"I remembered you mentioned wanting to see X-Men, so I got the tickets."

"I love how thoughtful you are." I felt bad for even thinking for a moment that he was out of line. He was a young man, and it was only natural for him to get a bit aroused by a woman in a sexy dress.

By the time we parked, got popcorn and other snacks, the movie was about to start. Halfway through the show, Jacob managed to put his arm around my shoulders, and for once, I started feeling like we were a couple. It was actually kind of nice.

"That was good," I said as we walked out of the theater.

"I think that might've been the best X-Men yet."

"Ditto to that."

"Are you hungry?"

"No, that popcorn and the two candy bars I ate are still resting on my stomach."

"Are you up to taking a ride?"

"It is a beautiful night and I'm in no hurry to get home, so why not."

"Then let's go."

I sat back in my seat with all the windows down, and the breeze felt wonderful. I almost wanted to tell Jacob to keep driving until we were in another world, or more like another state. The point is, for that brief time, all the sad feelings that had been weighing on my heart disappeared.

When Jacob began slowing down, I realized he was heading towards Grant Park. When he pulled up in front of Buckingham Fountain, all that pain that was gone came tumbling back. At one time this was me and Dalvin's special place, and now here I was with someone else.

"What are we doin' here?"

"I wanted to take you someplace romantic."

"Out of all the spots, this is the only one you could think of?"

"Why, what's wrong with here? Most people think Buckingham Fountain is gorgeous."

"You're right, it is. Don't pay me any attention."

"Well, that's hard to do with that dress you have on."

There it was again, the reference to my dress, but again, I tried to shrug it off. "So, are you lookin' forward to going back to school?"

"Am I making you uncomfortable with the comment I made about your dress?" he asked, picking up on my vibe.

"Maybe a little."

"I apologize. You're a very beautiful, sexy young lady, so it's hard to hold back."

"I guess I should be flattered. You've been such a gentleman."

"I would never want you to do anything that you didn't want to."

"Thank you, but there's something I do want to do if you don't mind." I leaned over and gave him a kiss.

"That was nice," he commented before reaching back over for another one.

This time he put his tongue into it, and I had to admit he was a good kisser. But I didn't see explosions like when I kissed Dalvin in this same spot the very first time.

"You're an incredible kisser, Mercedes."

"You're not so bad yourself."

Then, Jacob had to go in for the kiss one too many

times. As his lips touched mine, and as he used his tongue to pry open my mouth, my mind wandered off to Dalvin. The flashbacks of me wanting to have sex with him in his car at this park flooded my body. That night, my emotions got so caught up in Dalvin that I was ready to lose my virginity in the back of his Range Rover, not caring about consequences. The only thing that stopped me was Dalvin.

As Jacob got more aggressive with his kiss and put his hand on my thigh, I backed off. "Stop! This is all wrong!"

"What, do you want to go get a room or something?"

I didn't know if I should've felt offended by his statement, or guilty that I gave him the impression I wanted to give him some. "No, I don't want to get a room."

"Then what, you'll feel more comfortable in the backseat?"

Now he was working my last nerve. "How about you take me home, Jacob?"

"I don't understand. I thought you were feeling me like I'm feeling you."

"Yeah, I was feelin' you for a minute but..." my voice trailed off.

"But what?"

"This place has too many memories of me and Dalvin."

"You have got to be kidding me! You're still stuck on that guy? What's wrong with you? Your ex has moved on, and so should you."

I held my head down, feeling humiliated.

"He doesn't want you anymore, Mercedes, but I do."

"What, is that supposed to make me feel better?"

"It should. I'm a good catch. There are a lot of girls that would love to be in your place. Grown women too," he added to further stroke his own ego.

"Well, after you drop me off at home, go pick one of them up."

"I'm not dropping you off anywhere until you pay up."

"Excuse me?"

"I didn't skip a beat? You heard me. I've been playing Mister Nice Guy, so what, you can turn into some silly acting tease? Bringing you flowers, opening the doors, buying little gifts, and you think that was all for free? Naw, it doesn't work like that. I earned the right for you to come up out of those panties, and you can either do it voluntarily, or I can take it." In the blink of an eye, he had gone from the boy next door to the making of a future Scott Peterson.

"Forget about takin' me home, I'll call a taxi. Or better yet, I'll call my dad so I can tell him how you disrespected his daughter."

"Little girl, go running home crying to your daddy, but it'll be after I have my way with you."

Before I had a chance to react, Jacob had somehow got on top of me, pinned my arms down and leaned the seat all the way down. The pressure from his body weight had me gasping. His body was muscular, but it felt like an elephant was sitting on my chest. As he ripped at my dress, I was praying that someone would notice the commotion or hear my cries, but the place seemed deserted when we pulled up, and Jacob had turned the music up loud right before he attacked me. This had turned into the worst nightmare of my life, and I knew at that moment, only God could save me.

"What the hell are you doin'?" I heard a voice holler. Then an arm seemed to yank Jacob up like he was a rag doll.

The tears were now drenching my face, and I felt ashamed as I tried to cover myself. My dress was ripped up and my panties were halfway down my legs. Thank goodness Jacob didn't have the chance to enter me, but he was close enough.

By the time I looked up, my savior was giving Jacob the beat down of his life. He was slamming his head against the concrete and blood was splattering everywhere. I quickly saw that my savior was also the love of my life.

"Dalvin, that's enough! You're going to kill him!" His chest was going in and out at a rapid speed from breathing so hard.

Jacob was motionless. For a minute I thought he was dead, until I heard him mumbling through the blood that was trickling out his mouth.

After Dalvin calmed down, he came to me. "Baby, are you okay?"

"Yes, now that you're here. You saved my life. He was goin' to rape me."

"I know, baby, but he won't ever bother you again, I promise."

Dalvin then unbuttoned his shirt and put it on me so I would be covered up. He walked back over to Jacob and knelt down on the ground. "If you come anywhere near Mercedes again, I'll slice you up and toss your body parts across the ocean and feed you to the sharks!" He grabbed my hand and we walked back to his car. When we got inside, I just laid my head on his lap as he drove off.

"Dalvin, I'm so sorry!"

"What are you sorry for? You didn't do anything wrong."

"I should've never been out with him in the first place. If I had only stood up to my dad and fought harder for us to be together, none of this would've happened."

"Mercedes, you can't think about what you should've done, it's the past. You have to focus on now, and at this moment, we're together and that's all that matters."

"How did you know I was there?"

"I didn't. You know how I go to that spot to think when I have a lot on my mind? Since we broke up, I've been goin' there almost every night, tryin' to figure out how to make things right with you. When I saw the car, I didn't even know it was homeboy. At first I thought it was two people making out, but with the music being so loud, something didn't seem right to me. So, the closer I got to the car, I could see that the guy was forcing himself on the girl. It wasn't until I yanked him up that I realized you were the one he was attacking. Yo, I just lost it. If you hadn't of screamed out, I would've killed that guy with my bare hands."

"I'm glad that you didn't—I mean kill him. But I'm so happy you got me away from him. I love you so much, Dalvin."

"I love you too, never stopped. I'm so sorry for all the foul things I said to you that day at the fair. I was hurtin' and wanted to hurt you too."

"I knew you didn't mean it. I'm sorry for dating Jacob, but when I saw you with that girl, Sholanda, I was jealous and tried to use Jacob to forget about you. What a mistake that was."

"It's over with Sholanda. It was over before it even started. I hate that you even had to see me with her." Dalvin stroked my hair as he spoke to me, and it was so relaxing that I wanted to fall asleep in his lap. I hadn't felt this at peace since the last time he held me in his arms.

"Dalvin."

"What is it, baby?"

"I don't want us to ever be apart again."

"We won't."

"I mean it. I don't care what my dad says. I want to spend the rest of my life with you."

Instead of taking me home, he went to an apartment his family had in the city. He ran me a bath and I lay back relaxing as he gently lathered my body. When he finished, he carried me to the bed and held me while I fell asleep in his arms.

Chapter 12

Want You... Dead

When I woke up the next morning, Dalvin's arm was still wrapped around me. I breathed in the faint smell of his cologne that was still lingering on his skin. I started sprinkling his arm with light kisses.

"You sure you want to start that?" he mumbled, still half asleep.

"I'm positive. I've dreamed of you being inside of me again every day since the last time. I've missed you so much."

"I missed you too."

That morning, Dalvin and I made love again like it was our first time.

"Mercedes, am I hurtin' you?" Dalvin stopped right in the middle of his stroke when he saw the single tear rolling down my eye.

"No, baby, don't stop, you're not hurtin' me. That's a tear of joy. I can't believe you're making love to me again, and we're finally together."

"Oh, Mercedes, I won't ever let you leave me again. I put my life on that." I closed my eyes and held him tightly. I knew our love was so strong that only death could tear us apart.

After making love, Dalvin and I just held each other

for what seemed like a lifetime.

"Baby, it's time for me to go home."

"You sure you're ready?"

"I don't know if I'll ever be ready, but I have to face my parents. But I want to face them with you by my side."

"Are you serious?"

"Yes, unless you don't want to."

"Of course I want to, but I want to make sure that you're ready for this."

"I meant what I said when I told you that nobody would keep us apart, and that means my dad. I'm scared, that's why I need your support."

"You got that and anything else you need. We ridin' this out together, you and me."

"I love you."

"I love you too. Now you stay here. I'll be back in a few."

"Where are you goin'?"

"To get us somethin' to eat and you an outfit."

"You're the best."

"I try. I'ma take a quick shower and then I'm out."

"Don't leave me for too long."

"Never again." Dalvin gave me a kiss and went to take a shower. He left me with the biggest smile on my face, and nothing could wipe it off.

When he left, I got in the shower and spent the entire time going over what I would say to my parents, or more so to my dad. I didn't want another showdown, but I made up my mind that I would spend the rest of my life with Dalvin.

By the time I got out of the shower, Dalvin was back with breakfast food that smelled delicious.

"That food smells so good, or maybe it's because

I'm starving." I opened the white carton and poured syrup over the buttermilk pancakes. "These are delicious."

"I'm pleased you like them. I got you a couple of outfits. You can decide which one you're feeling."

Dalvin always dressed with impeccable style, but I was pleasantly surprised that it extended over to women's clothing too. I had to choose from a Marc Jacobs red and white polka dot dress with a vintage red patent-leather belt, or a chic pantsuit. I went with the dress. It was very girly, and I thought the perfect blend of innocence with a touch of confidence.

I finished eating my food and rushed to get dressed. I was anxious to get the whole ordeal over with. "I'm ready.

"You look incredible."

"It's because of you. Remember the dress you got me the first day we met? You know how to pick clothes that fit me perfectly."

"All I have to do is imagine your body in it, and the work is done."

"You're so silly."

"But honest. So, you ready, Bonnie?"

"You know it, Clyde!"

My Cell phone had been ringing all morning and hadn't stopped. It was Keisha and my parents, but I didn't want to talk to them until we were face to face. Dalvin and I held hands the entire time, and having him by my side made me feel a lot stronger. He was all I needed to stand firm.

When we pulled up to the gates, they opened as if another world was waiting for us. Dalvin parked the car, and I wondered if he could hear the pounding of my heart.

"Let's do this." I squeezed Dalvin's hand tightly as we walked side by side to the front door.

When we entered, I was expecting my dad to greet us with a gun aimed at Dalvin's head, but there wasn't a person in sight. I was somewhat relieved, but there was no doubt in my mind that it was about to go down.

"I wonder where everyone is."

We walked back to the kitchen and saw no one. We then heard the front door open.

"Mercedes, are you here?" I heard my mother yell out.

Dalvin and I went back to the foyer, and my mother and Keisha were still standing by the door. When they saw me with Dalvin, they both got the look of death of their faces.

"Hi. Where's Dad?"

They both continued to stand there, staring at Dalvin and me. That's when my dad came through the door, but the look on his face wasn't death, it was pure anger.

"Before you all say anything, I have to get this out. I'm in love with Dalvin, and God willing, we will be together for the rest of our lives. You guys are my family, and I don't want to lose you, but Dalvin is my future. If I have to choose between you guys and him, then I choose love."

"Have you been with him all night?" my dad asked.

"Yes I have."

"We were worried sick about you. I thought you were dead. You didn't answer your phone, and you didn't even call us. We've been out looking for you all day and night. This type of immature behavior is the main reason why I don't want you associating with someone like him. He brings out the worse in you."

Dalvin stepped forward about to defend himself, but

I pulled him back.

"Who would you like to see me with, someone like Jacob?"

"Yes, he's a lot more respectable than this thug, and he comes from a good family."

"I have to agree with Uncle Ronny, Mercedes. You never gave Jacob a chance because you were still caught up in Dalvin. Jacob was good for you, and he didn't come with a whole bunch of baggage," Keisha added.

After she finished, I turned to my mother, waiting for her input, but to my surprise, she remained quiet.

"Are you all finished singing the praises of a rapist?"

"What are you talking about?" my mother questioned with concern.

"That creep that you all keep goin' on and on about tried to rape me last night! Look at my dress!" I belted as I pulled out the ripped garments from the bag I had in my other hand. I tossed it at my family. "This is what that monster, Jacob did to me. If it wasn't for Dalvin, that fear you had of me being dead could've very well been a reality."

"I'll kill that bastard!" my dad kept repeating. My mother and Keisha ran up and hugged me.

"Mercedes, I'm sorry. I'm the one who pressured you to go out with that sick prick. I feel like such an idiot." My mother put her hand on the side of Dalvin's face and said, "Thank you for saving my daughter's life. I will forever be grateful."

"You don't have to thank me. I love your daughter, and there's nothing I wouldn't do for her."

"And, Ma, I love him too. Can't you please give us your blessing? You're the only mother I have, and I want you in my life, but I'm never lettin' Dalvin go again."

"You don't have to, Mercedes, you have my blessing."

"To hear you say that means the world to me."

"I don't care what your mother says, that boy will never be welcomed in my home or this family."

"Mr. Clinton, I know you've had business issues with my father, but I'm hoping we can put that behind us. I want to marry your daughter, and I know how much gettin' your blessing means to her. I'm willing to swallow my pride as a man and beg for your acceptance."

I knew how hard it had to be for Dalvin to say that to my dad, and it made me love him even more, which I didn't think was possible.

"You ain't a man, and I'll never accept you. Now get out of my house."

"Ronald, please stop. This young man saved our daughter's life, and she loves him. It should be clear to you that he loves her too. Let them be happy."

"Latoya, this is my house, and I want that boy out, now."

"Daddy, if he leaves, then I leave, and this time I won't be comin' back until you accept Dalvin."

"Mercedes, don't do this. We'll work it out. Your father is upset right now. He was worried sick about you, and when he calms down, he'll see things differently."

"No I won't. Boy, I'll see you dead before I ever let you live happily ever after with my daughter." My dad was now within spitting range of Dalvin, and the heat between them was burning me. Dalvin didn't flinch under the pressure. He remained stoic.

"Goodbye, Ma, bye, Keisha. I'll call you guys."

"Don't leave, Mercedes!" Keisha pleaded.

"I have to. I won't stay anyplace that Dalvin's not wanted."

"You're my baby. I can't let you walk out our lives."

"I'm not walking out your life. I'll be in touch. But until Daddy can stop being so stubborn, I won't stay here."

"Ronald, please do something! That's our little girl! We can't lose her!"

My dad said nothing as he watched us walk out the door.

"Beside the time I let you go, that was the hardest thing I ever had to do," I said to Dalvin as the door closed behind us.

"I know it was."

"But I don't regret one second. It was something I had to do. We belong together, and that's all that matters." I looked back at what used to be my home as Dalvin drove off. I had to let go of my past, because Dalvin was my present and future.

For the next few days, we stayed at the apartment in the city. Dalvin's parents wanted us to stay at their house, but after the last altercation, we decided that it was best if we didn't. We assumed my dad wouldn't think to track us down at the apartment. Virtually overnight, Dalvin and I started playing house.

The second day, we went to the grocery store and loaded up on food. To my dismay, Dalvin was a better cook than me. It seemed that he could do just about everything better than me. He never rubbed it in or tried to make me feel bad, but it did motivate me to step my game up.

One evening while we were sitting on the couch watching television, a back to school commercial came on, and I quickly remembered that my due date was nearing to return to my prep school. "Baby, I'm supposed to be leaving for school in less than a week. What am I gonna do? I'm sure my dad is goin' to cut me off financially now that we're living together."

"If you want to go back to your prep school, I'll pay for it."

"You'll do that for me?"

"Of course. I want to do whatever makes you happy."

"Being here with you makes me happy."

"In that case, they have a lot of great schools right here in the Chicago area. Pick which one you like, and I'll make it happen."

"What did I do to deserve you?"

"I should be asking you that question. So, are you stayin' with me or what?"

"You know it. I'll start looking into schools tomorrow. I'll also call my counselor at the prep school so they can have my transcripts sent here."

"Sounds like you have a lot to take care of tomorrow, so you get some rest while I head out."

"Where you goin'?"

"I have to handle some business. I've been laying up with you these last few days and completely slacked off on gettin' some things done for my father."

"I'm sorry."

"Don't be. They've been the best days of my life. Being with you is the only time I'm completely content."

"Really? You mean that?"

"You can't tell?" Dalvin reached over and put my hand on his chest. "Don't you feel how my heart beats when I'm next to you? That's what you call love, baby."

"You can't leave me after saying something like that. You're supposed to carry me upstairs and make passionate love to me."

"I'll wake you up when I get home later on tonight."

"You promise?"

Dalvin gave me that look like, you know better to even ask that question. "Let me get out of here. Hit me on the cell if you need anything."

"Besides needing you, I'm good."

Not wanting to, I finally released Dalvin from my embrace. I blew him a kiss as he walked out the door.

I turned the television off and was about to head upstairs, when I heard the sound of three shots ringing in the air. I rushed to the front door, fumbling to unlock it. My mind was racing, and I tried not to fear the worse. My hands were shaking, and I could hear other people coming outside to see what happened. This was an upscale, quiet neighborhood, one not used to hearing gunshots.

By the time I opened the door, there was a small group of people surrounding a body, so I couldn't see who it was. I noticed Dalvin's Range was still parked in the same spot from earlier, but in my mind, I made myself believe he took a cab. I heard the chatter among the crowd as each kept asking the other did they call the police.

The closer I got to the crowd, the more nauseated my stomach became. And when I finally reached the body, lying on the ground was my would-be future husband, face down with multiple shots in his back. Everything seemed to stop for me at that moment. The only thing I could hear was the blaring of my screams.

I had spaced out to the point that I didn't even realize that the ambulance had come until they physically removed me from leaning over Dalvin's body.

"Wait, I'm his wife! Can I please ride in the

ambulance with him?"

The paramedics looked at each other and nodded their heads for me to come along.

I remained silent, praying to myself that Dalvin wouldn't die. I had already made up my mind that if he didn't pull through, I would find a way to join him so we would be at peace together.

When we arrived at the hospital, they rushed him into the emergency room, but I wasn't allowed to go any further. As I waited, and during a brief moment of clarity, I called Dalvin's parents and told them he'd been shot, and I was at the hospital with him.

Mrs. Dewitt answered the phone, and I knew she was devastated, but she remained so composed. I had never met a woman in my life that always seemed to keep her cool under all circumstances. It amazed me. Here I was, about to have a nervous breakdown, and his mother was able to be more rational than I was.

When I hung up with Mrs. Dewitt, I called Keisha next. I needed her to be here with me. "Keisha, Dalvin's been shot!"

"What?"

"Yes. It happened less than an hour ago. We're at Northwestern Memorial Hospital. Please come. I need your support."

"I'm on my way."

When I hung up with Keisha, I went over to speak to a nurse at the front desk. "Any news on Dalvin Dewitt?"

"Are you a relative?"

"Yes, I'm his wife."

The nurse gave me a suspicious eye, probably because of how young I looked, but she opted not to interrogate me. "Miss, they're still operating. I won't know anything until they're done."

"Please let me know the moment you find out anything. I'll be right here waiting."

The nurse lovingly rubbed my shoulder, seeing all the pain I was in.

When I sat down on the chair and stared down at the cold floor, I saw that I didn't have any shoes on, just the socks I ran outside in. My eyes kept closing, and I kept hearing the gunshots in my head. Then I kept asking myself, Who would want to see Dalvin dead?

When I looked up, my mother, father and Keisha were walking in, asking somebody as to my whereabouts.

"I'm over here," I said to them.

"Baby, are you okay?"

"Do I look okay?" I stared down at my shirt and saw that it was drenched with blood.

"Are you hurt?"

"Besides my heart breaking, I'm alright. This is Dalvin's blood. Ma, somebody tried to kill him." I then looked up at my dad. "Did you have somethin' to do with this?"

"Mercedes, how can you ask such a question?" my mother asked, refusing to see the worse in my dad.

"You heard the threats that he made to Dalvin, just like I did. He said he would see Dalvin dead before he'd let us be happy. You remember sayin' that, don't you, Daddy?"

Dalvin's parents caught the last part of what I said, and without a word, Mr. Dewitt lunged at my dad. Hospital security quickly emerged on the scene, keeping the two men apart before it escalated any further.

"If I find out you had anything to do with the shooting of my son, I will have you buried alive!"

"Enough, sir!" the security guard stated to Mr. Dewitt.

"Get your hands off me! I don't take orders from you. Now move out of my way, I want to see my son." Mr. Dewitt walked over to the information desk with his wife right behind him.

"Daddy, how could you?" I banged my fist against his chest. "How could you try to kill Dalvin?"

My dad grabbed hold of my arms and held them firmly. "Baby girl, on everything I love, which means you, I'm not responsible for this. I know I made a serious threat in the heat of the moment, but when you walked out the door that day, I finally comprehended how much you love Dalvin. I didn't agree with it, but I would never harm him because I knew how much it would kill you. No matter what, you'll always be my baby girl. I couldn't do that to you."

"Oh, Daddy!" I broke down and cried, laying my head on his chest. "Daddy, if Dalvin doesn't make it, I just wanna die!"

My dad rubbed my back and cradled me in his arms. I understood then that this was what he had been trying to protect me from; the pain of falling in love with a man caught up in this life, and then losing him for the same reason.

When the doctor finished the surgery, he told us that there was a fifty-fifty chance that Dalvin would survive. If he made it through the night, then he was optimistic he would pull through.

We all stayed in the hospital, keeping a vigil for Dalvin. Mr. Dewitt refused to be anywhere near my dad, because although I believed he was telling the truth, Dalvin's father wasn't convinced.

His parents allowed me to stay in the room with

Dalvin, while everyone else stayed in the waiting area. For the next two hours, I sat right beside him with my hand resting on his, until I eventually fell asleep.

"Mercedes. Mercedes wake up."

For a minute I thought I was dreaming, until I heard a strained voice calling my name. I continued to sleep, but the voice didn't stop.

"Mercedes, baby, wake up."

I finally opened my eyes when I couldn't shake the calling any longer. That's when I saw Dalvin's beautiful eyes staring back at me. "Dalvin! I can't believe it! You're awake! Oh, baby, I was so scared." I stroked his face as I thanked God for letting him survive.

When the nurse walked in to check on him, I told her he was awake and to go get his parents.

"I'm happy I woke up and your face was the first one I got to see."

"I wouldn't have it any other way. I told all the staff that I was your wife."

"You are, but we're goin' to make it legal as soon as I get out this hospital. All we need is my parents' consent."

"Dalvin, you took ten years off my life with this one," Mrs. Dewitt said before giving her son a hug.

"Son, you had your old man worried. But you're a Dewitt, we can survive anything."

"I'm glad to be alive too, old man." They smiled at one another, as if sharing their own inside joke.

"Did you see who did this to you? Tell me, because they will be dealt with."

Dalvin stared at me for a moment, and my heart dropped. Was that his way of telling me that my dad was responsible? But my dad seemed so sincere when he denied being the blame.

"Was it Mercedes' father? If so, there's no sense in protecting him."

Dalvin looked at me and his father with a bizarre gaze. "No, it wasn't Mr. Clinton."

"Praise the Lord!" I sighed, finally able to exhale.

"Then who was it?" his father continued, determined to get to the bottom of this.

"Jacob."

My eyes got huge.

"You mean the boy that tried to rape Mercedes?" Mrs. Dewitt inquired.

After everything went down with Jacob, we told Dalvin's parents what he did to me, and how Dalvin saved my life. It never crossed my mind that Jacob would retaliate against Dalvin and try to kill him.

"He snuck up behind me wearing a ski mask. He caught me off guard, but I managed to pull off his mask before I went down. His face was still messed up from that beat down I gave him. It was Jacob, that's who shot me."

"Don't you worry, son, I'll make sure he never bothers you or anyone else ever again."

"Baby, I'll be right back. I want to speak to my parents for a second and let them know you're okay."

"Hurry back."

"Of course."

When I left Dalvin's room, my family was standing off to the side as if they had been waiting patiently for an update. "He's going to make it!" I smiled, running to give my parents and Keisha a hug.

"Girl, I'm so relieved. I got mad love for D."

"I know, and Daddy, I owe you an apology. Dalvin told us that Jacob was the one who shot him. I should've never thought it was you."

"Mercedes, I gave you every reason to think it was me. This potentially tragic incident with Dalvin made me put a lot of things into perspective."

"Me too, Ronald," Mr. Dewitt said, walking up to my dad. "My son and your daughter are very much in love. I'm sure we can both recall having those feelings. I married the woman that made me feel that way, and from what you told me a long time ago, so did you."

I caught my mother blushing.

"Why should we stop these two from sharing that also? I want to bury the hatchet. I'll do whatever it takes, even if it means handing over some of my territory to you, because my son's happiness is more important than any business deal."

"You don't have to do that. I want to bury the hatchet too. It seems we're going to be family, and family shares. What's mine is yours."

Both men reached out their hands, and something I never thought I would ever see took place right before my eyes. The two of them shook hands, calling a truce in their long-standing feud.

The very next moment, my parents and Dalvin's parents were talking to one another as if they had been friends all their lives. I practically leaped over to Dalvin's room, ecstatic to share the news.

"Why you grinning so hard?" Dalvin asked.

"Baby, we did it!"

"Did what?"

"Our love has made the impossible happen. Our fathers shook hands and called a truce."

"Word?"

"Yes, I witnessed it with my own eyes. The war

between our parents is finally over."

"Now when we get married, your dad can walk you down the aisle."

"That's music to my ears. I love you, Dalvin."

"I love you too, Mercedes."

Mercedes has been riding with Dalvin through all their obstacles but will their love endure the ultimate storm? Find out in...

COMING SOON...

A King Production
Order Form

A King Production
P.O. Box 912
Collierville, TN 38027
www.myspace.com/joyking

Name: _____

Address: _____

City/State: _____

Zip: _____

QUANTITY	TITLES	PRICE	TOTAL
____	Bitch	$15.00	____
____	Bitch Reloaded	$15.00	____
____	The Bitch Is Back	$15.00	____
____	Queen Bitch	$15.00	____
____	Last Bitch Standing	$15.00	____
____	Dirty Little Secrets	$14.95	____
____	Hooker to Housewife	$13.95	____
____	Superstar	$15.00	____
____	Ride Wit' Me	$12.00	____
____	Stackin' Paper	$15.00	____
____	Trife Life To Lavish	$15.00	____
____	Stackin' Paper II	$15.00	____

Shipping/Handling (Via Priority Mail) $5.50 1-2 Books, $7.95 3-4 Books add $1.95 for ea. Additional book.

Total: $_____ **FORMS OF ACCEPTED PAYMENTS:** Certified or government issued checks and money Orders, all mail in orders take 5-7 Business days to be delivered.

Joy (Deja) King

About the Author

Deja (Joy) King was born in Toledo, Ohio, and raised in California, Maryland, North Carolina and New Jersey. Ms. King represents a new breed of writers producing young, hip and sexy novels that introduce readers to street life in all its complexity and also takes readers behind the velvet rope of the glamorous, but often shady entertainment industry.

Ms. King attended North Carolina Central University and Pace University, where she majored in journalism. Emerging onto the entertainment scene, Deja accepted an internship position, and immediately began to work her way up the ranks, at The Terrie Williams Agency. She worked hands-on with Johnnie Cochran, The Essence Awards, The Essence Music Festival, The NBA Players' Association, Moet & Chandon, and other entertainment executives and celebrities.

Following a new chapter in her life, Ms. King attended

the Lee Strasburg Theater Institute before accepting a job as Director of Hip Hop Artist Relations at Click Radio, where she developed segments featuring the biggest names in hip hop. Ms. King pushed her department to new levels by creating an outlet that placed hip hop in the forefront of the cyber world.

Ms. King made her literary debut with *Bitch*, and followed it up with the bestselling sequel *Bitch Reloaded* and *The Bitch Is Back*. The saga continues with *Queen Bitch*. A prolific writer, King is also the author of *Dirty Little Secrets*, *Hooker to Housewife, Superstar, Stackin' Paper, Trife Life To Lavish* and *Stackin' Paper 2 Genesis' Payback* which she writes under her pseudonym Joy King.

For more information visit www.joykingonline.com and www.myspace.com/joyking